"I haven't seen you on the dance floor all night."

Pink colored Paisley's cheeks as she scooped up a plastic plate someone had left on the edge of the gift table. "That's because I've been working."

"Well, you know what they say about that."

She peered up at him.

"All work and no play makes Paisley a dull girl." As if she could ever be dull.

The slow notes of a guitar and fiddle began to play, so Crockett held out his hand. "Care to join me?"

For a split second, she looked nervous. Then one brow lifted in question. "I thought you didn't dance."

"I said I'm not much of a dancer. However, I can slow dance with the best of 'em."

After a long moment—long enough to have him second-guessing his decision—she smiled and placed her hand in his.

When they stepped onto the dance floor, he slipped one arm around her waist and pulled her close. Right where she was meant to be.

It took **Mindy Obenhaus** forty years to figure
out what she wanted to do when she grew up.
But once God called her to write, she never
looked back. She's passionate about touching
readers with biblical truths in an entertaining,
and sometimes adventurous, manner. Mindy lives
in Texas with her husband and kids. When she's
not writing, she enjoys cooking and spending
time with her grandchildren. Find out more at
mindyobenhaus.com.

Visit the Author Profile page at Harlequin.com.

A Future to Fight For

Mindy Obenhaus

LOVE INSPIRED
INSPIRATIONAL ROMANCE

LOVE INSPIRED®
INSPIRATIONAL ROMANCE

Recycling programs for this product may not exist in your area.

ISBN-13: 978-1-335-56715-4

A Future to Fight For

Copyright © 2021 by Melinda Obenhaus

This edition published by arrangement with Harlequin Books S.A.

For questions and comments about the quality of this book, please contact us at CustomerService@Harlequin.com.

Love Inspired
22 Adelaide St. West, 40th Floor
Toronto, Ontario M5H 4E3, Canada
www.Harlequin.com

Printed in U.S.A.

It is of the Lord's mercies that we are not consumed, because his compassions fail not. They are new every morning: great is thy faithfulness.
—*Lamentations* 3:22–23

For Your glory, Lord.

Acknowledgments

To my wonderful husband.
You are my hero, my best friend,
my biggest cheerleader and my greatest
blessing. Your love and support encourage me
beyond measure. Thank you for allowing me
to chase my dreams. I love you, always.

Chapter One

Excitement zinged through Paisley Wainwright like a hyperactive five-year-old jazzed on sugar. She was about to be back in the wedding planning business. And quite possibly as the owner of her very own castle.

How wonderful would it be to not only breathe new life into that deteriorating structure, but to boost the town's revenue with Blissful weddings and countless other events. What young woman didn't dream of being married in a castle? Bliss could become the wedding destination capital of Texas.

Settle down, darlin'. You're putting the cart before the horse.

With a firm grip on the steering wheel of her SUV and Lauren Daigle crooning from the speakers, Paisley drew in a deep breath and continued through the tree-lined streets of Bliss, Texas, Wednesday morning, attempting to rein in her euphoria. The Renwick family's attorney hadn't said a word about the family accepting her offer to purchase the castle their great-great-grandfather had built on the river in the late 1800s. Only that he wanted to meet with her today to discuss a proposition from the family.

But then, she couldn't imagine why he would come all the way to Bliss just to shoot down her idea of repurposing the structure and turning it into an event center.

The sun's rays peeked through the leaves of magnolia and live oak trees, greeting her as she parked alongside the courthouse square, across the street from Rae's Fresh Start Café where she was to meet Mr. Hollings at nine.

"Well, hello, sunshine. About time you decided to show up." They'd just come out of one of the rainiest Aprils on record and, based on the long-range weather forecast, the month of May wasn't setting up to be much better.

A morsel of trepidation squeezed her heart as she reached for her leather shoulder tote. What if the family had rejected her offer? What would she do then? After five years, her passion for creating fairy-tale weddings had finally returned, giving her hope for her future and filling her with a purpose that had been lacking for far too long. Sure, she loved her bed-and-breakfast, not to mention catering and providing baked goods for the café, but it just wasn't enough anymore.

However, Bliss wasn't Atlanta. Without the allure of Renwick Castle, business would be slow to say the least. People wouldn't want to come to Bliss for an ordinary wedding, and she didn't want to leave the quaint little town she'd come to think of as home. But something had to change.

One step at a time, Paisley.

Those five words had become her mantra since Peter and Logan's funeral. And she'd do well to remember them now.

As she reached for the door, a big black dually pickup truck pulled in beside her. Its diesel engine rumbled obnoxiously, and she wasn't too keen on the nasty-smelling exhaust either. Then she spotted the guy behind the wheel.

Crockett Devereaux. The one person in this world who seemed to look for opportunities to oppose her. The one who, just last night, single-handedly upended the renovation committee meeting at church. They were supposed to vote on either the sand- or the slate-colored carpet for the sanctuary. Until Crockett threw a monkey wrench into the works by suggesting they opt for wood-look tile instead.

She puffed out an incredulous laugh. Tile in the sanctuary? Not only was it expensive, the acoustics would be horrendous. Especially with more than half of the men wearing cowboy boots to Sunday service.

Yet when she'd politely pointed out that the cost would be double to triple that of the carpet, he'd narrowed his dark gaze on her and said, *As members of this committee, we owe it to the church to be good stewards of what they've entrusted to us. Tile will be more cost-effective in the long run.*

His smugness had her rolling her eyes so emphatically she almost strained a muscle. Had the man even considered the elderly congregants? Standing on that hard floor with their arthritic feet. It would only take one of them getting a bee in their bonnet over the whole thing and the entire lot of them would be headed over to Bliss Fellowship faster than they'd moved in years. Now, that was not cost-effective.

She heaved a frustrated sigh, knowing she shouldn't let the single father get to her. With an eight-year-old son and twelve-year-old daughter, the man was probably overwhelmed. What she couldn't understand was why he had it in for her. Like last year, when she was in charge of the church anniversary brunch and he insinuated a conflict of interest when she did the catering. Never mind the fact that she'd offered her services free of charge and convinced the grocery store to donate most of the food.

Tamping down her aggravation, she exited her SUV and slipped her purse over her shoulder before retrieving the baked goods from her back seat. Paisley provided cookies, pastries and other sweet treats for Rae's on a daily basis. It gave Paisley the opportunity to experiment with new recipes, and the townsfolk were always eager to scoop them up.

Unfortunately, Crockett rounded his truck just then, his scrutinizing gaze fixed on her. "You tryin' to topple your load?" He continued toward her.

"Hardly." Holding the three precariously stacked boxes, she managed to bump the door closed with her hip. The movement was just enough to have one of the boxes inching over the edge of the one beneath it. She gasped, trying in vain to catch it, but her hands were already full.

Gratitude warred with chagrin when Crockett intercepted it. He peered down at her. "Folks wouldn't be too happy if you spoiled their goodies."

At five foot ten, Paisley was anything but short. Still, she had to look up to meet the man's deep caramel eyes. As always, his sable hair was neatly trimmed and slightly spiked in all the right places with just a hint of gray at the temples, giving him a ruggedly handsome appeal.

Irritated her thoughts had drifted down such

an unwanted path, she squared her shoulders. "Thank you."

Scanning the series of Victorian-era brick buildings as they crossed the street, she drew in a breath, determined not to let him get to her. "Picking up your morning caffeine fix, I presume." Rae's was a daily ritual for many Bliss residents.

Balancing the box in one hand, he reached for the vintage wood-and-glass door with the other, motioning for her to enter. "I'm here for a meeting."

Inside the building that had once been a saloon, Paisley breathed in the enticing aroma of fresh-roasted coffee beans, wondering if she should order her usual nonfat cappuccino now or after her appointment with Mr. Hollings. She still had a few minutes.

"Good morning." Behind the antique wooden counter, Rae smiled, coaxing a wayward lock of brown hair back into her messy bun as they set the boxes down. "What tempting treats did you bring us today, Paisley?"

"Lemon melt-away cookies, pecan pie bars and caramel fudge brownies." She'd learned that if she didn't have at least one chocolate item in the mix it could lead to mutiny.

"Mmm." Rae's blue eyes sparkled with delight as she lifted the lid on the brownies.

"I'll have to pick up some of those cookies on my way out. Mac loves anything lemon."

Wait. Was that a hint of a smile on Crockett's face? Then again, his daughter was one of the sweetest twelve-year-olds in Paisley's Sunday school class. And there was no doubt that Mackenzie adored her father. Meaning Crockett must have some redeeming qualities hidden beneath that prickly exterior. Not that Paisley was interested in trying to find any of them.

Brow furrowed, he turned his attention to Rae. "I'm supposed to meet a Mr. Hollings. Can you tell me if he's here yet?"

All of Paisley's earlier anticipation congealed into one hard mass that now felt like a lead weight in the pit of her stomach. "I have a nine o'clock meeting with Mr. Hollings."

Crockett's slightly confused gaze narrowed on her. "Regarding?"

She stiffened. "That's none of your business."

Rae cleared her throat. "You'll both be happy to know that he's sitting right over there."

They turned as she pointed toward a table near the exposed brick wall opposite them, where a fair-haired gentleman, slightly younger than Paisley's forty-six years, looked rather out of place in khaki slacks and a navy sports coat. He stared at a tablet until he noticed them. Then he smiled, pushed out of his chair and started their way.

"Mr. Devereaux and Ms. Wainwright, I presume?"

They nodded.

The man extended a hand toward Paisley. "Doug Hollings."

She took hold. "Pleased to meet you."

He repeated the gesture with a seemingly irritated Crockett.

"No disrespect, Mr. Hollings, but why weren't we informed there would be others attending this meeting?" He cut a glance in Paisley's direction. As if she was happy about this.

"Frankly, Mr. Devereaux, this is a very unique situation." The attorney motioned toward the table he'd vacated. "If you'd care to join me, I'll be happy to explain."

They followed the man across the old wooden floor, weaving past empty tables, while the half dozen ranchers that gathered at the back of the restaurant every morning continued their lively conversation.

Crockett pulled out an industrial-style chair and gestured for Paisley to sit. She wasn't sure if he was ordering her or if he wanted to present a united front. But since she was just as curious as he was, she gave him the benefit of the doubt and sat.

A scowl marred his otherwise handsome face

as he eased beside her, his gaze fixed on the man across from them.

Mr. Hollings settled into his chair. "The Renwick family has never been approached about their great-great-grandfather's property before. And yet each of you reached out to them, expressing your interest within mere days of each other."

Paisley couldn't help looking at Crockett. Why would he want her castle? Was he planning to raze it and build something new? There was no way she would allow that gorgeous structure to be torn down.

Mr. Hollings continued. "That prompted the remaining heirs, Jared Renwick and Molly Renwick Simmons, to visit the castle."

Paisley's attention shifted his way. "They're here?"

"No. This was a month ago. Because of the comments both of you made regarding the condition of the structure, they wanted to evaluate things for themselves. Which brings me to the reason we're here today." He folded his hands atop the wooden table. "The castle is in a trust."

Crockett leaned back in his chair, crossing his arms over his broad chest. "In other words, the castle isn't for sale." He glared at the man. Much the way he had with her last night.

"That is correct."

Paisley gripped the edge of her chair, her heart breaking as her dreams of weddings and a Blissful Christmas at the castle shattered into a million tiny pieces, right along with her future.

"However—" Mr. Hollings's single word dangled before them like a lifeline "—given the passion each of you have shown with your detailed plans for the structure, they would like to extend a counteroffer."

Paisley's hopes fluttered back to life. "What kind of offer?"

"They would like to name both of you as directors to oversee the renovation of Renwick Castle."

"You mean, we'd be working together?" Incredulity had her voice lowering a notch.

"Yes, and that is one of the family's stipulations. In part because it's a large undertaking and also the dual administration lends itself to greater accountability. The family will finance the project, however they will also have final approval on all changes and upgrades."

Crockett shifted in his seat, apparently no more comfortable with the idea than she was. "I appreciate that they trust Ms. Wainwright and myself with what will, no doubt, be a major project. But how will this benefit us? After all, we each had our own plans for the castle."

While Paisley was curious to know just what

Crockett's plans were, she also found herself grateful that he was here. There was strength in numbers. Particularly when they had a common goal.

"Of course. And the family has taken that into consideration. Matter of fact, they were quite impressed with each of your proposed ideas. So, in return for your services, you will both be given exclusive rights to use the castle as a museum—" his gaze shifted from Crockett to Paisley "—and an event venue."

She almost giggled out loud. Her dream had been revived. The castle would be open for weddings. Granted, the addition of a museum wasn't ideal, but she supposed the structure was big enough to support that and still leave plenty of space for countless marvelous events. There was just one problem. And his name was Crockett Devereaux.

Crockett didn't think this day could get any worse. First his computer crashed while Mac was attempting to print her English homework, then David spilled chocolate milk down the front of the class shirt he was supposed to wear for today's field trip to the exotic animal ranch outside of town. Even though Crockett managed to locate Mac's old shirt from when she was in Mrs. Pomeroy's class, David still had a meltdown. All because hers was red as opposed to his bright blue one. Then, when they finally made it out the door, the plant manager at Devereaux Sand and Gravel called to let him know his wife had gone into labor, meaning Crockett had to head over to the plant as soon as he finished here.

Now the Renwicks wanted him to work alongside Paisley Wainwright?

Uh-uh. Not happening. They couldn't even make it through a church committee meeting without butting heads. The castle would take months to renovate. Evidently the fact that his grandfather had been the caretaker of the castle for nearly forty years hadn't scored him any points.

He ran a hand over his face, pondering the woman beside him. Of all the people who could have expressed an interest in Renwick Castle, why did it have to be Paisley? He didn't dislike her, however his ex-wife had left him with a strong aversion to women who looked like models, had big houses and even bigger dreams. Sure, it probably wasn't fair, but that knee-jerk reaction was there, nonetheless.

So, the thought of sharing the place where he'd hoped to showcase his collection of Texana artifacts, memorabilia and historical documents didn't settle well.

"I don't suppose we could go look at the castle,

could we? Go inside?" Paisley's sugary Southern drawl jarred him from his thoughts. Her long, copper-colored hair was gathered into a braid that swept over one shoulder. Throw in the stylish jeans and blouse, and she looked as though she belonged in Dallas or Austin, not Bliss.

"Of course," said Mr. Hollings. "As a matter of fact, I'm looking forward to seeing it myself." Grinning like a kid on Christmas morning, he gathered up his paperwork and tablet. "I've brought a list of items the family would like to see addressed, so perhaps we could go over that while we're there."

Paisley's sapphire eyes turned to Crockett. "Care to join us?"

Crockett was tempted to say no. If the family wasn't interested in selling, what was the point? But then he'd sound like a spoiled child who hadn't gotten his way. Besides, it had been decades since he'd been inside.

As a kid, he'd spent his summers in Bliss with his grandparents, and Papaw always let Crockett tag along when he went to the castle. Once there, Crockett's imagination had run wild with visions of knights, kings and, as he got older, a beautiful princess locked away in one of the castle's towers.

He looked from Paisley to Mr. Hollings. "I'm ready when you are."

They headed for their respective vehicles and caravanned across town.

To his surprise, Crockett's anticipation swelled with each block. He'd been pondering his grandfather's dream of turning the castle into a museum for years. Then one day, as he was crossing the river bridge, the castle caught his eye, and all those childhood musings came flooding back. What better place for his Texas history collection than inside a unique piece of Texas history?

Renwick Castle would draw more than just history buffs, though. Curiosity seekers of all ages would come to Bliss. They'd eat and shop here, helping local business owners. And once the media got ahold of the news that there was a castle in Bliss, there was no telling how far things could go. But sharing the castle had never been a part of his plan. And given the value of his collection, he found the idea unsettling.

Nearing the castle, he noticed that much of the view was obscured by the sprawling limbs of ancient live oak trees and the kudzu that covered the limestone walls surrounding the structure.

Crockett parked on the side of the road before joining Mr. Hollings at the gate. "I think the first thing we're going to need is a landscaper." He plucked some of the vines from the metal gate while the attorney fumbled with the lock.

"Does that mean you're willing to share?"

He twisted to see Paisley moving toward them. "What?"

Smiling, she cocked her pretty head. "You said 'we.'"

"There we go." The rusted gate squeaked as Mr. Hollings pushed it open. "Oh, wow." He paused just inside, his gaze traversing the three-story limestone structure with a rounded tower at each corner. "This is most definitely a castle."

"Technically, it's a castellated mansion." Crockett moved beside the seemingly confused man. "We're just not that big on technicalities around here."

"What Mr. Devereaux is trying say is that this is a residence built in the style of a castle—" standing on the opposite side of the attorney, Paisley continued "—with the towers and battlements." She pointed out the square openings along the edge of the roof. "Whereas a true castle is a fortress."

Crockett peered around the other man to stare at the woman. "You've done your research."

"Actually, I spent some time in Europe."

Of course, she had. Her whole life had probably been gilded. Just like his ex-wife's.

Mr. Hollings looked from Paisley to Crockett. "Sounds like you two know your stuff."

As they continued up the drive, toward the stone portico surrounding the front door, Crockett couldn't quell his excitement. His heart raced as he took in the gothic-arched windows along the towers and the Scottish coat of arms carving over the entrance. "Angus Renwick had all of this limestone brought down the river from Austin." The words seemed to bubble out, as if he couldn't contain them.

"That was convenient." Again, Mr. Hollings fumbled with the keys.

"Not to mention faster and more cost-effective than bringing it in by wagon," Paisley added.

A thrill skittered through Crockett the moment Mr. Hollings pushed open the large wooden door, stealing his breath. Renwick Castle was not only unique, it was inspiring. Born of a passion, it seemed to urge others to dream, too.

"Looks awfully dark in there." Hollings was hesitant to say the least.

"I'll be right back." Crockett brushed past them, moving into the vestibule before continuing into the drawing room to his right. He threw the heavy brocade drapes aside with a whoosh, then crossed to the opposite side of the hall to the library and repeated the move.

Paisley and Mr. Hollings entered as he returned, their mouths agape as they took in the stone walls and mahogany wainscoting.

Paisley lowered her gaze to the stone floor. "It's more rustic than I'd imagined. Like a Texas/

medieval mashup—" Suddenly, she let out a scream.

"What on earth…?" Crockett followed her line of vision, noticing a mouse fleeing to safety. "Seriously?" He narrowed his gaze on hers. "All that noise for a little mouse?"

She stiffened her spine. "He startled me."

Mr. Hollings coughed as he eyed the knight's armor standing sentry at the edge of the hall. "It's quite dusty in here." He removed a white handkerchief from his hip pocket and covered his mouth.

"That'll happen when a place is closed up for more than three decades." It'd been thirty-five years since his grandfather closed the doors on this place for the final time. Crockett was twelve. And to his knowledge, no one had been here since. Until the Renwicks' recent visit.

Crockett lifted his gaze to the tall, coffered wooden ceiling that spread toward the back of the house, eager to continue. He strode the length of the hall, past the wooden staircase that stretched up the wall to his right and threw open the drapes, sending dust motes into the air. Even with a haze coating the tall windows, the view of the swollen river was spectacular.

He repeated the move with the remaining three windows, his pulse racing as sunlight filtered through the massive trees that stood between the terrace and river. "This is what I remember most."

"What do you mean, 'remember'?" Paisley came alongside him with Mr. Hollings in tow, her attention drifting to the view. "Oh, my." She pressed a hand to her chest. "This is stunning."

Crockett opened the French doors, humidity washing over him as he stepped onto the stone terrace with Paisley on his heels. "Just think what this must have looked like when Angus built the place. There were no dams along the river back then, so it would have stretched even wider."

"Can you imagine the wedding photos?" Exhilaration filled Paisley's voice.

"Yes, this is quite nice." Mr. Hollings used his handkerchief to blot his brow.

Crockett looked across the weed-filled, overgrown yard, recalling the beautiful gardens his grandfather had been determined to maintain even though no one lived there.

"I can hardly wait to see the ballroom." Paisley hurried back into the house.

"Hold up." Crockett followed her inside and made a quick right turn. "Follow me." He continued to an opening at the base of the corner tower where he used to pretend he was a knight storming the castle.

"A secret passage!" Paisley all but squealed. "Oh, this just keeps getting better and better."

Catching Doug Hollings's wary eye, he said, "You coming?"

"Of course."

Crockett led them up the winding stone steps, feeling as though he was ten years old again. Of course, back then these steps hadn't seemed quite so narrow.

When they emerged on the second floor, they continued into the ballroom where Paisley squealed with delight, like the proverbial kid in a candy shop. She promptly went to work opening the drapes along two walls, oohing and aahing over the view, the once-glittering chandeliers and the massive fireplace.

"And would you look at these floors."

Coming alongside her, he observed the inlaid wood that covered the space where he and his grandfather would have mock sword fights. "They'll need to be refinished."

They continued to the third floor where Paisley declared the six bedrooms perfect for bridal parties preparing for weddings.

When they finally returned to the first level, Mr. Hollings excused himself and went outside for some fresh air while Crockett showed Paisley the outdated kitchen, the dining room and a space akin to a family room with an old console television and furniture from the 1960s.

"You sure know your way around this place," she said. "Have you been here before?"

"My grandfather was the caretaker of Renwick Castle. When I'd visit, he'd bring me with him."

"That must have been quite a treat."

"It was. Especially for a kid with an active imagination." Uncomfortable with talk of his personal life, he strode back into the entry hall. He could envision his collection in each of the first-floor rooms. There was a fair amount of natural light, but extra LED lighting would be needed.

He looked at Paisley. "You want to turn this into an event venue?"

"Yes. With that ballroom, the possibilities are endless. Parties, Blissful weddings, a Blissful Christmas. The town could use it for all sorts of things."

He couldn't miss the emphasis on Bliss. At least helping the community was something they could agree on.

"And what's this about a museum?" Crossing her arms, she eyed him suspiciously.

"Texas history. I have an extensive collection that's overwhelming the climate-controlled barn I built to house it in."

One perfectly arched brow lifted. "That must be quite a collection."

"It is."

She slipped her long fingers into the front pockets of her jeans. "What do you think about the Renwicks' offer?"

Eyeing a nest something had built in the corner, he said, "There's a lot of work to be done here. Aside from general repairs, cleaning and landscaping, we'd have to upgrade the air-conditioning, maybe electrical and plumbing." He refrained from telling her the house originally had wood pipes. "And everything would have to be ADA compliant, so there'd need to be an elevator to provide access to the second and third floors."

She pointed toward the back of the house. "That tower to the right would be perfect for an elevator."

Seemed she had an answer for everything. "Sounds like you're completely on board with this."

"Why wouldn't I be? I still get my event venue and, if I'm understanding Mr. Hollings correctly, it won't cost me a thing."

She had a point there. Except things were personal for him. He'd spent his entire life building his collection. Had items passed down from his grandfather and great-grandfather. So to have people moving in and out of the castle when the museum wasn't open... Well, that didn't sound any more appealing than working with Paisley.

"It won't cost you either." Her sapphire eyes

bored into his, challenging him on more levels than he cared to admit.

"That's where you're wrong. Because it could cost me a lot more than I bargained for."

Chapter Two

I can't believe I'm doing this. But Paisley needed to know where Crockett stood.

She aimed her SUV up the long tree-lined drive at Crockett's ranch late the next morning, with more butterflies in her stomach than she'd had on her wedding day. At least marrying Peter Wainwright had been a sure thing. But whether or not Renwick Castle would be put into her care hinged on Crockett. And after seeing the inside of the castle yesterday, she wanted it so badly she could taste it. If only Crockett felt the same way.

She understood his desire to protect his collection, but she couldn't help wondering just how extensive it really was. After all, there were countless Texans who took pride in their state and had accumulated lots of trivial tokens—just nothing the average man on the street cared to see. And if she lost out on Renwick Castle because Crockett was worried about a bunch of minutiae...

Easy, girl. This is not the time to let your temper get the best of you.

Relaxing her grip on the steering wheel, she followed the paved drive as it curved toward the single-story lodge-style home perched atop a hill. It wasn't a huge house, but the wall of windows that stretched to the two-story center peak certainly made for an impressive entrance.

She eased to a stop beside a camo utility vehicle parked in the circle drive, turned off the engine, grabbed the box of baked goods from the passenger seat and shot up a prayer.

Lord, please let Crockett agree to this deal. And help me to hold my tongue, even if he rubs me the wrong way.

With that, she sucked in a breath and exited her vehicle.

Gray clouds drifted overhead as she continued on to the sweeping flagstone porch, her insides all aflutter. If Crockett wasn't willing to share the castle, she didn't know what she would do.

Thanks to stories like "Cinderella," "Snow White" and "Sleeping Beauty," Paisley had been dreaming up fairy-tale weddings for as long as she could remember. It's why she became a wedding planner over a dozen years ago. Weddings by Paisley had built a reputation as one of the top event designers in all of Georgia. Then her own happily-ever-after was snatched away. Her passion was gone, right along with Peter and their ten-year-old son, Logan.

Turning, she looked out over the pastoral setting, her gaze landing on a pair of horses savoring the lush green grass. Over the past year, after catering several receptions and helping two of her friends plan their nuptials, her passion had rekindled. She'd come to the realization that, even though her happily-ever-after had slipped through her fingers, she still wanted to be the fairy godmother that made others' wedding dreams come true.

Suddenly, the door opened behind her.

"Is there something I can help you with?"

She whirled to see a cranky Crockett glaring at her. Her gaze moved from his scowl to the maroon Texas A&M T-shirt that hugged his muscular chest and biceps.

Gripping the box in her hands, she said, "I had some extra lemon cookies." Extending the package toward him, she continued. "I thought Mackenzie might like them. There are some caramel fudge brownies, too. David couldn't seem to get enough of them at the last church potluck. And then, just for good measure, I threw in some of the molasses cookies I baked this morning." Ugh! She hated it when she rambled.

He looked from her to the box and back again.

"You wouldn't be trying to butter me up so I'll agree to the Renwicks' deal now, would you?"

Drat. He was onto her.

Shifting from one sandaled foot to the next, she said, "You mentioned yesterday that Mackenzie loved anything lemon. And, well, I couldn't very well leave David out."

"And you just happened to make molasses cookies today, not realizing that they're my favorite."

She gulped. "They are?"

He nodded. "My grandmother used to make them for me. They bring back fond memories."

Great, now he thought she was trying to bribe him when the cookies were simply an excuse. "Well, I hope mine taste as good as hers did." She shoved the box into his hands. "And I'm not trying to butter you up. I was simply curious if you'd made a decision yet."

"No." Did he always have to be so blunt?

"Okay... Can you tell me why?"

"I'm not sure I'm comfortable showcasing my collection in a place that will be used for other purposes, with people traipsing in and out when I'm not there."

Crossing her arms, she pinned him with a stare of her own. "Tell me about this collection."

He worked his jaw, his dark eyes narrowing as he seemed to ponder her request. "As long as you're here, I'll just show you." He gestured to the box. "Let me put this inside."

As he disappeared into the house, she moved back to the drive, the rapid-fire chatter of a cardinal making her smile as she took in the gorgeous vista. Rolling hills stretched as far as she could see. Some wide-open, others wooded. Oh, to be able to pull up one of these rocking chairs lining the porch and simply stare out over such a peaceful setting.

The front door opened, and Crockett appeared again. "We'll take the Ranger." He pointed to the utility vehicle that had a front and back seat, along with a small cargo bed.

Following him, she couldn't help noticing he was eating one of her molasses cookies. "So, how are they?"

He nodded as she climbed into the passenger seat. "They pass muster." Popping the last bite into his mouth, he said, "Don't forget your seat belt."

Determined not to allow his less-than-glowing review to get to her, she buckled up.

Crockett hit the gas and started away from the house. In no time, the paved road turned to gravel and two large metal structures loomed ahead. She knew from talking with Mackenzie that they not only had horses but boarded and trained them, as well.

"Is that part of your training facility?" She pointed to the larger building that was open on three sides.

"The majority of it, yes."

Gathering her hair in her hand to keep it from whipping in the wind, she looked at him. "Are you a trainer?"

"No. The facility was here when I bought the place. The previous trainer agreed to stay on, so I decided to keep it going."

"What do you do, then?"

"I'm a gravel guy. My company quarries raw materials from a number of places around the region."

Eyeing the lush green pastures dotted with horses and a charming faded red barn, she could only assume gravel was lucrative. "You've got some spectacular views out here."

Crockett came to a stop in front of a smaller building tucked behind the two larger ones. "That's why I bought the place." He stepped out of the vehicle.

"How many acres do you have?" She unbuckled and followed him to the door of the metal building that resembled a large garage.

"Couple hundred, give or take." He unlocked the dead bolt, then punched a code into the keypad near the handle. Finally, he pushed open the door and stepped inside, turning on the overhead lights as he went.

Warehouse-style shelves stretched from front to back, each holding some sort of container. Wooden boxes, plastic tubs, metal lockboxes… She glanced from the large worktable near the door to a framed poster of the Alamo on the far wall. Turning, she noted a historic Republic of Texas map—a replica, she was certain—over the table.

"It's quite comfortable in here." Not to mention clean. Even the concrete floor was pristine. "I thought it would be hot."

"No, sirree. Not with these antiques." He pointed toward one wall. "This building is insulated and climate-controlled to ensure that the humidity is low, and the temperature remains between sixty-eight and seventy-five degrees year-round."

"I see."

He moved to one of the shelves and retrieved a wooden box. He set it atop the table and removed the lid to reveal a tarnished sword. "This—" he withdrew it from its container "—belonged to Santa Anna and is believed to have been used in the Battle of San Jacinto."

Paisley lifted a brow. "Wasn't he at the Alamo, too?"

He gave her a harsh look. "Sounds like somebody could use a Texas history lesson."

"Funny, they didn't cover that in Georgia."

Over the next hour and a half, he passionately revealed artifacts and historic documents relating to Texas history. Cherished pieces from Texas's early years, including a cannon that had been used at the Alamo and a letter written by Stephen F. Austin, along with other items ranging from the cattle boom in 1870s to the oil boom in the early 1900s and countless items in between, none of which were trivial as she'd expected.

"Where did you get all of this stuff?" She watched as he carefully tucked the last box away.

"Some of it was passed down from my grandfather who'd inherited several things from his father." He moved to another shelf and removed a cloth covering to reveal a scale model of the Alamo. "Papaw and I built this when I was a kid. It's a replica of how the Alamo would have looked in 1836." Replacing the covering, he continued, "Of course, I've acquired a good many things on my own, too."

"You must have started young, then, because there's a lot here."

"Over thirty thousand pieces at last count."

"That's amazing." She dared to look him in the eye. "I'm quite impressed. This is not at all what I expected. You obviously have a fervor for Texas history."

He lifted a shoulder. "Guess I come by it honestly. Davy Crockett was my great-great-great-great-uncle."

She felt a slow smile coming on. "You're messing with me now, aren't you?"

"Not at all." His expression was so serious.

"Is that why your folks named you Crockett?"

"Yes, ma'am. My father was adamant that if he ever had a son that'd be his name."

"And is that why your son is David?"

He nodded. "David Crockett Devereaux."

"Why not Davy?"

He shook his head. "That's not what they called my uncle. Some playwright dubbed him Davy Crockett after his death and, unfortunately, it became forever linked with his folk hero persona. Just like the coonskin cap."

Her mouth dropped open. "You mean he didn't wear a coonskin cap?"

"Not once."

"Well, if that don't beat all." She surveyed the space, her heart twisting. "Thank you for showing me all of this. Now I understand your concern. Not only is your collection valuable, it's sentimental."

"That it is."

At least he had a good reason. Not that it made things any more palatable. Because without Crockett, her castle dreams were no more.

* * *

Dark clouds churned overhead as Crockett drove his pickup through the streets of Bliss with his kids later that evening. He'd hoped enchilada night at La Familia would get him out of the funk he'd been in all afternoon. But despite a full belly, his unease lingered.

He should not be feeling bad for Paisley. Yet, ever since she left his place earlier today, he'd been beating himself up. If he didn't agree to the Renwicks' deal, her plans for the castle were dead in the water.

Why had the family proposed an all-or-nothing deal anyway? It wasn't fair to him or to Paisley. Because even though she might not be one of his favorite people, he didn't want to stand in the way of her dream. He wasn't that callous, especially after she'd taken such an interest in the items he showed her, asking questions and, seemingly, understanding his apprehension.

"Slow down, Dad." From behind him, Mac enthusiastically patted his shoulder. "There's Ms. Paisley!"

His gaze shifted to the corner lot just ahead. Yep, there she was in her side yard, crouched beside a lawn mower.

"Hi, Ms. Paisley." His daughter all but hung out of the now-open window, waving as they approached.

Standing, Paisley smiled and returned the gesture as he continued past the stately Victorian.

"What are you doing?" Annoyance filled Mac's voice.

"Trying to get us home before this storm hits." He pointed to the sky. Definitely more threatening than the patchy clouds that had been there when they came into town. Then again, it was spring in Texas where weather could turn on a dime.

"You can't just leave her there." In the rearview mirror, Mac's dark eyes pleaded with him.

"Why not? She's already home."

"But she needs help."

"And how do you know that?" Glancing at the mirror, he was met with the dreaded eye roll.

"Dad, it was so obvious. A person doesn't just stare at their lawn mower." Crossing her arms, she flopped back in her seat. "You're supposed to be a gentleman."

His grip tightened around the steering wheel. "Mac, it's about to storm."

"I don't care."

Still eyeing the mirror, he looked to David sitting behind the passenger seat.

His blue eyes glimmered. "She brought us cookies and brownies, Dad. You should help her." He nodded adamantly.

Traitors. They could forget about enchilada night next week.

Crockett made a U-turn then rounded the corner and pulled into Paisley's driveway, wondering why a single woman would want such a big house. Then he glimpsed the sign hanging in the yard. Blissful Bed and Breakfast. He'd forgotten about that.

Twisting to face his children, he said, "You two stay put. This shouldn't take long." At least he hoped not.

"But, Dad, we need to thank her for the cookies." Mac already had her door open, and David was unbuckling his seat belt.

So much for quick.

Shaking his head, Crockett killed the engine and followed them as thunder rumbled in the distance.

"What a pleasant surprise." Paisley smiled as his children pushed through the gate of the vintage iron fence that wrapped around the yard.

"We wanted to thank you for the cookies." Mac hugged her Sunday school teacher. "They were so good."

"The brownies were even better, though." David's snaggletoothed, bashful smile was priceless.

Crockett's heart twisted. While he was doing his best to be both mother and father to Mackenzie and David, times like this reminded him of all the little things they were missing out on without a female influence in their lives. It wasn't so bad for David, he supposed, since he barely remembered his mother, but Mac struggled sometimes, especially now that she was about to be a teenager.

Crockett rubbed the back of his neck. Shannon had done a number on all of them, following in the footsteps of his own mother. How a woman could simply walk away from her family was something he'd never comprehend.

"I'm glad you enjoyed them." Backdropped by a leafed-out crepe myrtle, Paisley wiped sweat from her brow with the back of her hand. "How is school going?"

"It's so boring." His twelve-year-old gave an exaggerated eye roll, then quickly brightened. "But we only have two weeks left."

"And what do you plan to do with your summer?"

Mac's smile went wide as she tucked a strand of brown hair that had escaped her long ponytail behind her ear. "Whatever I want."

Crockett couldn't contain his chuckle. "That's highly doubtful, young lady. At least, not if you still want to earn some money."

His words set off yet another eye roll. The

wind kicked up as she leaned toward Paisley. "I have to muck stalls."

"Oh, I see." Paisley pressed her lips together as though trying not to laugh. "Well, maybe once you've saved some of that money, we can go to the city and do some shopping."

The girl's expression brightened. "Really? Do you mean it?"

"Of course, I do. But we'll need to make sure it's all right with your father."

He eyed the two, recalling all the times Mac had been let down by her mother. He wouldn't let Paisley do that to his daughter.

A peal of thunder echoed across the sky, quickly followed by another, reminding him why they were there.

He looked at the woman whose long copper hair was piled on top of her head. "Are you having a problem with your mower?"

She nodded. "I don't know what's wrong. It was running fine, then it sputtered and died."

"Does it need gas?"

Her I'm-not-stupid look was accentuated by a gust of wind.

Clearing his throat, he said, "Mind if I take a look?"

"Be my guest."

Kneeling beside the mower, he checked the spark plug and throttle. Nope.

Sprinkles peppered his arms as he turned the machine on its side. Thick green clippings spilled out while more lodged around the blades, likely impeding their movement. Setting the mower back on the ground, he glanced around the small yard, noting the thick St. Augustine grass. With all the rain they'd had this spring, the stuff was growing like gangbusters.

Standing, he said, "When was the last time you mowed?"

"Five days ago. And I need to get it done because I have two rooms booked for this weekend."

Thunder crashed over their heads, making Paisley shrink while Mac and David latched on to Crockett's waist.

Smoothing a hand over David's back, he eyed the blackening clouds. "Looks like things are about to let loose." He looked from Paisley to Mac. "We need to go."

"Of course." Paisley had to raise her voice to be heard over the wind.

"No, Dad." Mac gripped his arm. "What if there's a tornado and your truck is flipped over?"

"Mac, plea—"

A brilliant flash accentuated by a crack of thunder had all of them ducking.

Both Mac and David whimpered as Crockett

locked gazes with a wide-eyed Paisley. "That was too close for comfort."

"That's for sure." Turning, she waved them toward the back of the house as the rain began to pour.

While the kids rushed ahead with Paisley, he grabbed hold of the mower and hurried behind them.

Paisley tucked the kids inside then sprinted to the detached garage and opened the door so he could stow the machine.

When he emerged, she looked up at him. "Thank you. I appreciate you doing that."

For a moment, he simply stared at her. He'd never seen her so…unadorned. Between the simple work clothes, the rain and the heat, she looked like anything but a fashion model. And she was downright gorgeous.

Forcing himself to look away, he said, "Wind's picking up. We don't need any projectiles out there."

Another loud clap of thunder had her jumping.

"We'd better get inside." His hand instinctively fell to the small of her back, urging her out from under the eave and into the onslaught of wind-driven rain. The gesture sent a shot of heat racing up his arm.

He quickly pulled back as moisture penetrated his T-shirt and jeans.

Ahead, he saw Mac holding the door open, frantically motioning for them to hurry.

As they neared the covered porch, the hairs on the back of Crockett's neck stood on end. They had to get inside.

He propelled Paisley toward the door then dove behind her, landing hard on the porch's wooden floor. Air rushed out of his lungs as lighting so bright it hurt his eyes flashed around him, accompanied by an instantaneous and deafening boom that sounded as though a high-caliber gun had been fired next to him.

From inside, he heard Mackenzie scream. David cried.

Crockett dared a glance through the railings to see leaves and twigs raining down. Then a distinctive snap ripped through the air, sending a chill up his spine.

He covered his neck and head with his hands as a low groan gave way to a loud crash. The sound of breaking glass added to the cacophony as a rush of wind, rain and debris swept over him.

When the racket dissipated, he pushed to his feet, brushing leaves from his hair as he noted the massive tree limb that now stretched across the drive, burying his truck beneath a sea of bright green leaves. His muscles tensed. *Thank You, Lord, that my children weren't in there.*

He turned his gaze to the still-open door, an eerie silence enveloping him. Shards of glass and leaves littered the wooden floor. And his children were nowhere to be found.

Chapter Three

"Is it over?" Mackenzie's bottom lip trembled as she stared up at Paisley with those beautiful caramel eyes.

Inside of her small pantry, Paisley and the kids had huddled together while nature had its way with her house. She didn't know if it was a tornado or something else, but she was grateful God had prompted her to shelter Mackenzie and David in the tiny space. Simply hearing the chaos had been frightening enough.

She hugged Crockett's children closer. "I hope so."

But with the sounds of the storm quieting bit by bit, one question drowned out every other thought: Where was Crockett? She thought he was right behind her. Now she prayed he was all right.

"Mac! David!" Crockett's panicked cry boomed like the thunder that had finally subsided.

His daughter scrambled to her feet and pushed open the pantry door. "Daddy!"

He hurried toward her. "Praise God you're all right."

She leaped into his arms and hugged him tightly. "I was so scared."

"I know you were, sweetness."

The loving exchange warmed Paisley's heart. To her surprise, though, David remained snuggled against her, his body shivering. She cinched him closer and continued to stroke his short brown hair with her fingers, just the way she used to do with Logan. He'd never been a fan of storms either.

Crockett set Mackenzie to the floor and held her hand as he continued toward the pantry. Crouching in the doorway, he rested his elbows on his knees. His hair and clothes were soaked.

Tenderness filled his eyes as he studied his son. "You okay, buddy?"

The boy nodded against her shoulder. But when he looked up at her, she saw a tear streaming down his cheek.

Her heart melted right then and there. Smiling at the frightened little boy, she wiped away his tear with her thumb. "He was very brave."

Crockett straightened and moved into the space. "Come here, son." He scooped the boy into his arms before extending a helping hand to Paisley.

Warmth infused her when his fingers touched hers. As he pulled her to her feet, she looked into his dark eyes. "Are you all right? You weren't hurt, were you?"

"I'm fine." He abruptly let go and turned into the kitchen. "Though I can't say the same for your house and my truck."

Following him, she said, "Why, what happ—?" The words lodged in her throat when she looked across her kitchen to see a tree where windows had once been.

"Whoa…" David squeezed his father's neck.

Shock sifted through Paisley as her gaze traveled from the window to the table and the floor. The entire kitchen was littered with glass and leaves.

She pressed a hand to her stomach, trying to quell the sudden roiling. If she and the kids hadn't taken shelter, they'd be tending wounds instead of gawking at the wreckage.

"I'm so glad we were in the pantry." Mackenzie wrapped her arms around Paisley.

"Me, too, darlin'." Slipping one arm over the girl's shoulders, she tilted her head to look at Crockett. "Was there a tornado?"

"Lightning strike. Took a big ol' chunk out of that oak tree beside the drive." He shifted David to his other arm. "If you think it's messed up in here, just wait till you see the outside."

That was all the impetus Paisley needed. Releasing Mackenzie, she picked her way across her war zone of a kitchen, until she reached the back porch where she promptly traded her sandals for a pair of rubber boots.

She had guests arriving tomorrow night for this weekend's Bliss Barbecue Fest. How would she ever get this mess cleaned up by then?

One step at a time.

With thunder rumbling to the east, she squared her shoulders. That's right. Everyone was alive and well, and that was all that mattered. Besides, the upstairs rooms were all ready to go, so—

Terror rushed through her. What if that limb broke the upstairs windows, too?

Ignoring the sprinkles dotting her bare arms, she hurried to the corner of the house to survey the second floor, relief washing over her when she saw that the upstairs windows were still intact.

Thank You, Lord. And thank You for protecting us.

Crockett and his children approached as her scrutiny moved to the limb that was nearly a foot in diameter.

"Looks like I'm going to need a chain saw." She brushed the hair out of her face. No doubt she looked a complete mess.

While the kids examined the hefty branch, Crockett screwed up his face. "You know how to use a chain saw?"

Memories of helping Peter clear trees from the property they'd owned back in Georgia played across her mind. Happy memories of working together as a team. It had been more fun than work.

"I sure do."

"Well, I need to call my ranch foreman to come and pick us up, so I'll tell him to bring a couple with him."

"A couple?"

"Two of us working will speed up the process. It's already getting late, and it'd be good if we could at least get that top part out of your window."

"Most definitely. Though I'll need to come up with some plastic or wood to cover the openings." If it wasn't so late, she'd run over to Bliss Hardware. Christa, the owner, would know exactly what she'd need. But with the store closed and her recently married friend living out in the country, Paisley would have to improvise until morning.

The sun hovered over the western horizon as Crockett pulled out his phone and dialed. "Carlos. Hey, buddy."

While Crockett wandered back toward the house, Paisley eyed the rapidly clearing sky. Popup storms like this one were all too common this time of year. Though, until now, she'd never suffered any damage.

"Paisley, dear."

She turned to see Margaret Matthews, her neighbor from two doors down, moving toward her as quickly as her blinged-out flip-flops would allow.

"I'm so glad you're all right." The seventy-something blonde hugged her for all she was worth. "That lightning like to have scared the livin' daylights out of me."

Margaret's husband, Bruce, let out a low whistle as he approached. "You're gonna have a doozy of a time tryin' to get rid of that limb." He looked puzzled as he stopped beside his wife. "Whose truck is that?"

Paisley pondered her response. Margaret was the biggest gossip in all of Bliss, and Bruce ran a close second. If they thought there was anything even remotely going on between Paisley and Crockett, word would be all over town by morning.

Crockett's children abandoned their exploration of the tree limb and joined her.

"Have you met Mackenzie and David Devereaux?" Paisley looked from Margaret to the kids.

"Is Crockett your daddy?" Bruce eyed Mackenzie and her brother.

"Yes, sir." Mackenzie squinted as the sun reappeared in the western sky.

"Fine fellow." Bruce nodded his approval.

"Handsome, too." Margaret's bright pink lips lifted into a knowing smile, right along with her drawn-on eyebrows.

"Mackenzie is in my Sunday school class." Paisley fingered the girl's long ponytail. "She stopped in to say hi, didn't ya, darlin'?"

"I came, too." David puffed out his little chest.

"And I'm so glad you did." She gave his shoulder a squeeze.

"Well," said Bruce, "looks like their little visit put Crockett's truck in the wrong place at the wrong time."

Paisley winced at the broken windshield and dented hood. "That's for sure."

Toothpick sticking out of his mouth, Bruce removed his hands from the pockets of his baggy cargo shorts long enough to point toward the house. "I see you got some windows busted out there, too."

As if that was news to her. "Sure enough."

Out of the corner of her eye, she spotted Wayne Larsen, another neighbor, crossing the street.

"Little lady, you've got quite a mess over here." She smiled at the kindhearted man who had the energy of someone half of his seventy-five years. "Just thought I'd do a little remodeling."

He chuckled. "Why don't you go ahead and take some pictures for your insurance before it gets too dark. I'll go grab my chain saw so we can get that window cleared for you." He turned his attention to Bruce. "You've got a chain saw, don'tcha, Matthews?"

Hands back in his pockets, Bruce shuffled his feet. He had no interest in helping. He was only there to gawk.

"But it's getting dark." Margaret set a hand to her chest, feigning concern as she peered at the rapidly clearing sky.

"Even more reason to jump on it now." Wayne left no room for argument.

"All right, Carlos will be here as soon as possible with a couple of chain saws." Crockett stopped beside her, still staring at his phone.

"Already got it covered."

As if suddenly realizing there were other people there, Crockett jerked his head up. "Hey, Wayne." The two shook hands.

"That your truck?" Wayne pointed.

"Unfortunately." The word came out as a sigh.

"Looks like you're going to have a little trouble gettin' home."

"'Fraid so." Crockett rubbed the back of his neck as he eyed Wayne. "My foreman is on his way to pick us up. You say you've got a chain saw, though?"

"Yep. Let me go grab it, and we can get to work." Wayne turned to Bruce. "Matthews, you get yours, too. If you don't want to dirty your hands, we'll let ol' Crockett here use it. 'Cause the faster we get this taken care of, the better off Paisley will be." Grinning, he sent a wink her way.

She loved Wayne's take-charge attitude. No wonder he was her favorite neighbor.

After she took pictures of the damage with her phone, the men set to work outside while she and the kids went into the house. The poor things. Aside from all of the stress, it was nearing their bedtimes. Lord willing, Crockett's foreman would be here soon, and they could head home.

In the meantime, she settled the children in front of the television in the living room where they'd be able to relax. Well, however relaxed one can be with the sound of chain saws buzzing outside the window.

Still wearing her rubber boots to protect her feet, she set to work in the kitchen, armed with a broom and dustpan. Since the men were working around the window, she started on the main part of the kitchen, clearing debris from the floor and countertops.

Once the countertops were cleared, she wiped them down with bleach. She'd still be baking for Rae in the morning, so she wanted things clean and ready to go. Thankfully, the electricity hadn't gone out.

Taking a break, she checked on the kids. Mackenzie had made herself comfortable in the recliner while David was stretched out on the sofa. A second glance revealed that he was asleep. The poor thing had had a tough night.

After covering the boy with a blanket, she returned to the kitchen as Crockett came in the door.

"How's it going out there?" She couldn't help noticing that at least half of the tree had disappeared from the window.

"That's coming along fine. But I have another problem."

Grabbing the broom and dustpan she'd leaned against the counter, she waited for him to continue.

"Carlos called. The road is closed because of a downed power line. He can't get through."

"That's not good." She worried her bottom lip.

They could stay here.

When pigs fly.

"If you can clear a section of that log from the driveway so I can get my vehicle out, I could drive you home."

He frowned. "No way out means no way in either."

"Good point." Her brain must be muddled. She should have realized that.

Bending, she swept another pile of debris into the dustpan.

"I'll see if Wayne can run me and the kids over to the Bliss Inn. Hopefully, they've got a room."

Are you really going to let them do that?

Why not? If Crockett Devereaux was here all night that would give Margaret Matthews all sorts of fodder for the rumor mill.

"Where are the kids?" Sawdust peppered his dark hair and clung to the sweat on his tanned face.

"Living room." She emptied the pan into the heavy-duty trash bag next to the island. "David is asleep." Meaning Crockett would have to wake him to go to the motel.

"Poor kid." Crockett frowned.

She corralled another heap onto the pan. "He was pretty stressed during the storm." *And yet you're ready to wake him up and send him out into the night.*

"Daddy, when is Carlos going to be here? I'm tired."

Paisley straightened to face Mackenzie, who was standing in the doorway between the kitchen and the entry hall.

"He's not." Crockett explained the situation.

"Then where are we supposed to sleep?" His daughter pouted.

"I'll see if—"

Her conscience getting the best of her, Paisley cut him off. "You'll stay here."

"Awesome." Mackenzie bounced on the balls of her sneakers.

Yet, while she seemed pleased with the idea, Crockett looked at Paisley as though she'd lost her mind. "Huh?"

Obviously, he wasn't any happier about this turn of events than she was. But there was no turning back now.

"Mackenzie, you take the small bedroom at the top of the stairs." She dared a look at Crockett. "You and David can share the one across the hall with the king-size bed."

"I'm gonna go look." Mackenzie took off for the stairs.

Dragging a hand through his hair, Crockett said, "I don't like this idea."

As if Paisley was thrilled about it. "Why not?"

"Because people might talk." He pulled his phone out. "I'm calling the Bliss Inn."

"Fine. If you want to haul your sleeping son out into the night and disappoint your daughter, go right ahead." That might have been a low blow, but she didn't care. She was weary and getting crankier by the moment.

"Yeah, well, you should have checked with me first before saying anything in front of Mac."

She set the broom aside and stepped in front of him. "Uh-uh, no way am I going to let you guilt me on that. I get that you're frustrated about your truck, which is why I extended the offer in the first place. So don't you dare fault me for being gracious."

He puffed out a laugh. "The kids won't have any clothes for school in the morning."

"Oh, and they have clothes at the Bliss Inn? At least I have a washer and dryer so the clothes they do have can be cleaned."

"Dad—" a beaming Mackenzie clutched the moldings around the doorway " you aren't going to believe this. I get to sleep in a canopy bed. You have to see it."

As Mackenzie scurried away, Paisley turned her attention back to Crockett. "You still going to make that call?"

He didn't say a word. Instead, he shoved his phone into his pocket and marched back outside.

He needed to get out of here.

With his son sleeping peacefully beside him, Crockett stared into the darkness of Paisley's guest room. He shouldn't be here. He didn't want to be here. He should be in his own bed, in his own house. And if he'd continued on home after dinner last night the way he'd intended, that's exactly where he'd be. Sound asleep, not plagued by thoughts of how Paisley had protected his kids and how she'd rolled up her sleeves and set to work cleaning the mess in the kitchen, all while making sure everyone else's needs were met.

The woman had grit. That not only surprised him but had him contemplating agreeing to the castle offer. Except that would mean working with Paisley on a daily basis, just the way they had last night. He wasn't sure he could handle that.

It was midnight by the time they got the windows covered. A tarp and some duct tape were the best they'd been able to come up with, and it had taken teamwork to get the job done. Funny how neither of them really said a word yet seemed to anticipate each other's moves.

The enticing aroma of coffee stirred him from the traitorous thoughts and had him slipping out of the bed. He donned his jeans and T-shirt before padding down the steps in his bare feet. Halfway down, he recalled all of the glass on the kitchen floor last night. He should have grabbed his boots. Then again, Paisley had meticulously cleaned things, going over the space with a vacuum several times after the broom.

Reaching the bottom step, he caught the scent of more than just coffee. Paisley was baking? He glanced at his watch. Five thirty. Had the woman been up all night?

He moved through the entry hall into the kitchen where a large pan of something with coconut and chocolate chips sat on a cooling rack atop the marble-topped island, while blueberry muffins were perfectly lined up next to it on a second rack.

"Good morning." Paisley rinsed her hands at the sink opposite the island. She wore a long T-shirt over skinny jeans, and her red hair was again piled on top of her head, though a few loose strands framed her face.

His mind still muddled from lack of sleep, he sent her a curious look. "How long have you been up?"

Turning off the water, she grabbed a towel from the counter. "Since four." She was operating on only a few hours of sleep.

"Why?"

"Because I have a commitment to Rae. And I have a lot to do today to get ready for my guests tonight."

He watched her drape the towel over the oven handle to her left, feeling like an underachiever. "I need coffee."

Opening an overhead cupboard, she retrieved

a red-and-black mug before reaching for the carafe on the coffee maker near the sink. "Cream or sugar?" She handed him the oversize cup.

"Cream, if you've got it." He noted the University of Georgia emblem and mascot on the side of the mug as she moved past him to open the refrigerator. "Bulldogs, huh?"

"My alma mater." Closing the door, she handed him the creamer. "Do you have a problem with that?"

"Nope." He added a couple of splashes to his brew then accepted the spoon she pulled from a drawer on the island. After giving the liquid a quick stir, he set the spoon aside and picked up the cup to savor the invigorating scent. "You from Georgia?" He took a sip.

"Born and raised." She retrieved a mixing bowl from a cupboard under the island.

"So how'd you end up in Bliss, Texas?"

Slowly straightening, she cut him a quick glance before setting the bowl on the island. "I was ready for a change of scenery."

While she moved to the refrigerator to pull out butter and eggs, he wandered toward the table where his kids' clothes were neatly folded and stacked. Paisley had given each of them a T-shirt to sleep in last night so she could wash their things for school today.

Looking over his shoulder, he surreptitiously

watched as she skillfully set to work on another recipe. From all appearances, she had a good work ethic. Not at all like Shannon, who preferred to spend her days shopping or lunching with friends.

Paisley's determination would make her an asset in renovating Renwick Castle.

What? No, he was still concerned about the security of his collection. She knew that.

"In case I forgot to tell you last night—" Paisley interrupted his thoughts "—thank you for helping me with the windows." She nodded toward their patch job behind the table.

"It was the least I could do after you gave me and the kids a place to sleep." He stared into his now half-empty cup. "Besides, I owe you a debt of gratitude, as well. You protected my kids when I wasn't able to." He looked at her now. "Thank you."

Nodding, she smiled and focused on stirring whatever it was she was making. Cookies, maybe? "They're good kids."

"I think so. They have their moments, but—" Emotion clogged his throat, preventing him from saying anything more. For the umpteenth time, he was reminded that if Paisley hadn't sheltered Mac and David in her pantry, they could have been at the hospital right now instead of tucked upstairs, safe and sound.

Yeah, he owed her a lot more than a patch job on her windows, all right. And he wasn't sure how he felt about that. Trust didn't come easily for Crockett. Especially when it came to women.

He'd seen the way Mac and David looked at Paisley. They were both taken with her, kicking his protective instincts into high gear. He'd been the one to pick up the pieces of their broken hearts after Shannon left, and he still recalled the sting of watching his own mother toss her bags into the back of that old blue pickup truck and drive off without so much as a goodbye. She hadn't cared about him any more than Shannon cared about Mackenzie and David. And Crockett was not about to let his children be hurt again.

Looking around the magazine-worthy kitchen, he suddenly wished he could escape.

Instead, he studied some framed photos scattered among several decorative pieces on an iron rack near the table. Paisley was easy to recognize with her red hair. There was one of her and a man sharing a loving embrace. Aware that she was a widow, Crockett assumed that was her late husband. Then there were pictures of her with a red-haired boy who looked to be a little older than David. Her nephew maybe?

"Cute kid." He pointed as she lifted her head. "His hair's the same color as yours."

Her movements stilled as she looked away. "That's my son. Logan."

Son? Crockett wasn't aware she had a son.

She reached for a towel, wiping her hands as she approached him. "He died in the same car accident that took my husband." Stopping beside him, she continued. "He was ten."

Speechless, Crockett simply stood there, feeling as though he'd been punched in the gut. How does one overcome something like that? Losing a spouse to death would be hard enough, but to lose a child at the same time? He couldn't even begin to fathom the amount of strength it must take for her to get up every morning knowing that they weren't there.

Looking down at her, he could see the sorrow in her eyes. Yet, there were no tears.

He felt like a heel. "I—I'm sorry, Paisley. I had no idea."

"I know you didn't." She tilted her head to meet his gaze, her smile tremulous. "That's why I told you."

Could that be why she'd needed a change of scenery? "How long ago?"

"It'll be five years next month." Making her son a few years older than Mackenzie, had he lived.

Reminding himself to give his kids extra big hugs this morning, he searched Paisley's face, her peaceful expression, realizing just how wrong he'd been about her. She had an inner strength and determination he wasn't even sure he possessed.

"I'm sorry you had to go through that."

She nodded. "Me, too. But God is good, and I firmly believe that He has a plan and a purpose for everything, good or bad." Her tone left no room for argument.

How was that possible? She'd lost her entire family, not to mention all of the hopes and dreams that went along with it. Something he could relate to, though on a different level. Yet, there wasn't a hint of anger or self-pity in Paisley's words.

While Paisley returned to her work, her statement had him taking a hard look at himself. He knew what God's word said, believed most of it, yet he still struggled with bitterness, especially where his mother and ex-wife were concerned.

"By the way—" Paisley pulled two large baking sheets from a cupboard and set them next to her bowl "—since seeing your collection yesterday, I've been contemplating security measures that could be implemented to ensure its safety."

He felt the corners of his mouth lift. "You're kidding, right? I mean, with everything else going on…" He gestured toward the window.

Pulling what looked like a small ice cream

scoop from a drawer, she chuckled. "This was before the storm." She began scooping balls of dough onto the baking sheet. "You said you're looking at using primarily the first floor of the castle for the museum, correct?"

"Yes." He dropped into a chair and mentally shifted gears.

"Most of the rooms on that level have solid wood doors, so they should be quite easy to secure. They would simply need some industrial-strength locks and, of course, security cameras throughout that level." She set the first tray aside and started filling the next. "But the drawing room, which is open with pillars, would need to be fortified somehow."

"That's the largest room, too. And the opening is a good twelve feet wide."

"Indeed." She opened the oven door before taking hold of the two pans with the cookie dough. "What if we put in some of those accordion-style metal gates?" She set the pans in the oven and closed the door. "Of course, they'd need to go to the top of the opening so no one could climb over, but when the museum is open, they could be pushed against the walls so as not to detract from the beauty of the castle." Brushing a lock of hair away from her face, she continued. "But we'd need to make sure the Renwicks would be all right with us drilling into the walls to secure them."

He couldn't help staring, in part because he was stunned that Paisley had put that much thought into the security of his collection, but also because he couldn't believe he hadn't thought of something along those lines first.

"That's not a bad idea," he said.

One eyebrow arched. "Not bad? I thought it was quite brilliant myself." She grabbed a pink mug from the counter and took a sip before joining him at the table. "Look, I know the Renwicks' offer is a lot different than either of us were anticipating. But given the fact that we're both passionate about preserving the castle and using it, and that we were actually able to work as a team last night, I think we should put aside our pride, adjust our dreams—" she lifted a shoulder "—and go for it."

As a businessman, he respected that she was willing to cut to the chase. And he had to admit, the fact that she not only understood his concerns about the security of his artifacts but had come up with some viable measures to overcome his objections impressed him. But there was still one part of the equation he wasn't sure of, and that was working with Paisley. Could she be trusted?

It was a business relationship, not a marriage proposal. Plus, he was starting to realize that when it came to business, Paisley was no amateur. Her ideas were well thought out, with a great deal of passion behind them—not merely a flash in the pan as he had first believed.

He considered her once more. The woman had guts. He could appreciate that. He supposed there was only one thing left to do.

Stretching his hand across the table, he said, "Ms. Wainwright, I believe you've got yourself a deal."

Chapter Four

Under a canopy of live oak and magnolia trees, Paisley meandered the lawn around the courthouse square Saturday evening alongside her very pregnant friend Laurel, who was pushing her two-year-old daughter, Sarah-Jane, in a stroller. The near perfect weather had more than half of the town and dozens of visitors turning out for the Bliss Barbecue Fest.

Children gravitated toward carnival games on the east side of the courthouse while a country band played a toe-tapping tune on a stage to the south. The aroma of smoked meat carried on the breeze, stirring Paisley's appetite.

She breathed deep, savoring the opportunity to spend time with her friends. A couple of years ago, she, Laurel, Rae and Christa had been practically inseparable. Now that Laurel and Christa were married with families, it was more difficult to find a time that worked for everyone. But with Laurel's husband, Wes, taking part in the barbecue competition, this was the perfect occasion for a little girl time.

"So, you're really going back into the wedding business?" Laurel waved to one of the older ladies from church.

"I sure hope so." Paisley eyed some homemade lavender soap in one of the vendor booths. "For now, though, I'm concentrating on bringing Renwick Castle up to par."

"Paisley, you are the only person I know who could have pulled off a coup like that. I mean, that place has been sitting there gathering weeds forever."

"I know, and it was so sad to see it deteriorating when it had the potential for so many wonderful things."

"Are you sure you're going to be okay sharing it with Crockett Devereaux, though? I mean, you two are kind of like oil and wat—"

"Ms. Paisley!"

She lifted her head, smiling when she saw Mackenzie hurrying toward her with three friends in tow. "Hey there, sweet thing." She returned the girl's hug before eyeing the group. "Are you girls here all by yourselves?"

"Uh-huh." A bubbly blue-eyed blonde tittered.

"We're waiting to do the climbing wall." Taylor Bennett, a no-nonsense brunette from Paisley's Sunday school class, informed her.

"That sounds like fun."

"It is so fun." Another girl with shoulder-length sandy-brown hair beamed. "And everyone wants to do it."

Focusing on Mackenzie, Paisley said, "Did your father get his truck repaired?"

"Yeah. The windshield, anyway. He says the dents can wait."

"That's goo—"

The third girl grabbed hold of Mackenzie's arm. "The line's getting longer! We need to hurry."

The other girls nodded emphatically.

"In that case, y'all have fun."

"We will." Mackenzie waved as they departed, her long, dark ponytail swishing back and forth.

Returning her attention to Laurel, Paisley shook her head. "Did we have that much energy when we were their age?"

"Probably." Laurel's honey-blond waves spilled over her shoulder as she handed her daughter a small bag of fish crackers. "Which means I'm in no hurry for Sarah-Jane to grow up."

"I still can't believe she's going to be a big sister." Wyatt James was slated to make his debut in early July, and Wes was beside himself. He hadn't learned about Sarah-Jane until she was fourteen months old, so the experience was all new to him.

Paisley's gaze roamed the crowd until she spotted Rae moving toward them at a brisk pace. "About time you got here," Paisley said as she hugged her friend.

"You guys aren't going to believe this." Breathless, Rae pulled away.

"Believe what?" Laurel gave the woman her full attention.

"I just got off the phone with a caseworker." Rae's blue eyes sparkled as she brushed a lock of brown hair away from her face. "They're bringing me two children tomorrow."

"That's wonderful!" Paisley's heart swelled as Laurel high-fived their friend. Rae had talked about becoming a foster mom for over a year. Now, with all of the paperwork, background checks, home visits and training behind her, she was finally going to have two little ones to dote on and love beyond measure. "Those kids are going to love you."

Rae's excitement could hardly be contained. "I sure hope so."

"What are their names?" Laurel rested a hand atop her ever-growing baby bump.

"I don't know yet. They only told me that the girl is six and the boy is five." Rae blew out a shaky breath. "And that their homelife has been pretty bad."

"That just breaks my heart." Paisley pressed a hand to her chest as though she could somehow quell the ache.

"Mine, too." Rae nodded.

"I'm just glad they'll have you to show them unconditional love," Paisley said.

Rae lifted a shoulder. "I hope it's enough."

"Ms. Paisley! Ms. Paisley!"

The cries had her whipping around to see two of Mackenzie's friends rushing toward her, their faces red with panic.

"What is it, girls?" She set a hand on Taylor's shoulder.

"It's Mackenzie." The girl gasped for air. "She's hurt."

Paisley glanced at her friends.

"You go on." Rae waved her away. "We'll catch up."

Paisley followed the girls through throngs of people and into the street that had been closed to traffic until they reached the rock-climbing tower. At the base, a man hovered over a whimpering, helmet-and-harness-clad Mackenzie.

Concern had Paisley pushing past onlookers to get to Crockett's daughter. "What happened, darlin'?" She knelt beside the girl.

"My ankle." The girl hiccupped.

"I don't know what happened," the thirty-something man said. "She climbed just fine."

"Did you hurt it while you were climbing?"

Mackenzie shook her head. "I'm so stupid. I lost my balance trying to get out of my harness."

"Now, now, we'll have no name-calling." Paisley wrapped an arm around the girl's waist and lifted her onto her good foot. "You are not stupid. You simply lacked grace for a moment."

That made Mackenzie smile.

"I'm afraid you're not going to be able to stay out here, though." She helped the girl out of her harness while the gentleman removed her helmet. Meeting Mackenzie's dark gaze, she continued. "We need to get some ice on that foot and keep it elevated. When is your father picking you up?"

"Not until eight."

Paisley checked her watch. It wasn't even six. "Let's find someplace for you to sit down, then I'll call your father." She looked around to see Rae and Laurel approaching. "Laurel, grab that table." She pointed across the street. "Rae, come help me, please."

With Mackenzie's arms around their shoulders, they helped her to a chair while the other girls followed. Paisley called Crockett, but there was no answer.

Looking at Mackenzie, she said, "Why don't you try him? See if he answers."

Mackenzie did as Paisley asked, with the same outcome. "He's probably still in the horse barn. Dad says the metal building makes our phones not work sometimes."

"I see." No telling how long he'd be in there. And while she didn't think Mackenzie had broken anything, she did want to take the necessary precautions. "If I could figure out a way to get you to my house…"

"You could take me home." Mackenzie flashed her a hopeful smile.

"I have guests, darlin', so I need to stay close by."

"I don't mind monitoring things at your place." Rae grinned. "Matter of fact, it'll give me an opportunity to see what sort of baked goods you have on hand so I can pilfer some for the kids tomorrow."

"My sweet friend, not only are you welcome to take whatever you want, but I will gladly make you a fresh batch of chocolate chip cookies in the morning."

"Deal."

Paisley looked at the girls surrounding their wounded friend. "All right. Y'all keep her company while I go get my vehicle."

Almost an hour later, she pulled her SUV into

Crockett's drive. As she neared the house she saw him exit one of the big barns with David at his side.

"Looks like you called it, Mackenzie." She eased to a stop in front of the house as the guys hopped on the UTV and started toward them.

Seconds later, Crockett pulled alongside her, confusion pinching his brow as she exited her vehicle.

"Hi, Ms. Paisley." David scrambled to undo his seat belt, looking genuinely happy to see her.

"Hello there." She smiled as he hopped out to hug her around the waist.

"What are you doing here?" Crockett was coated in dust and sweat from his black Dickies T-shirt to his well-worn jeans, and he definitely didn't look happy to see her.

"Bringing your daughter home."

Mackenzie opened the back door on the driver's side. Paisley had put her back there along with a pillow and ice pack so she could elevate her foot.

Her father whisked past Paisley to get to his girl. "What happened?"

"I twisted my ankle." While Paisley thought the girl might cry at the sight of her dad, she remained calm.

Crockett promptly scooped her into his arms

and started toward the house. "Why didn't you call me?"

"We tried, but you didn't answer. I told Ms. Paisley you were probably in the barn and asked her to bring me home."

He glanced over his shoulder as he pushed through the wood-and-glass front door. "You were at the festival?"

"Good thing, too." With David at her side, Paisley followed them into the house, through a nondescript foyer to a large room that encompassed the living, dining and kitchen areas. "Mackenzie's friends sought me out after she injured herself."

While Crockett settled his daughter on the overstuffed leather sofa, Paisley's gaze drifted from the vaulted ceiling to the wall of windows that overlooked a pool and a view even more spectacular than the one in front of the house.

Straightening, Crockett stared at Mackenzie. "So what happened?"

"Dad, it was so embarrassing. I'm such a klutz."

Paisley lifted a brow. "Young lady, what did I say about calling yourself names." She turned her attention to Crockett. "She stumbled trying to get out of her harness at the climbing wall."

"Lindsay and Callie laughed at me." Mackenzie pouted. "Until they saw me crying."

Crockett eased onto the sofa. "They don't sound like very good friends to me."

Paisley watched as he examined the girl's foot. "I don't think anything is broken, but it's likely to be tender for a while."

"Yeah, I think you're right." He eyed Mackenzie. "The swelling doesn't seem to be too bad."

"Ms. Paisley gave me an ice pack to put on it."

He pushed to his cowboy boot–clad feet. "Good idea. I'm about to fix you another one."

While he did that, Paisley moved beside the girl. "All right, darlin', you stay off that foot and do what your daddy tells you."

"Yes, ma'am. But I still want to come to church tomorrow. Maybe I'll be on crutches." The idea alone seemed to add an expectant gleam to Mackenzie's dark eyes.

Paisley regarded Crockett as he approached with the ice pack. "I'm going to head on back to town."

"I'll walk you out." He eyed his son. "David, you keep an eye on your sister."

"Cool!"

Paisley chuckled as they made their way outside. "I'm guessing David doesn't get to be in charge very often."

"As if Mac would allow that." Pausing near her SUV, he said, "I appreciate you bringing her home."

"Not a problem." She continued toward the driver's door. "You know, we should get together sometime this week to go over our list of expectations for the castle. The Renwicks' attorney will be sending the contracts soon, and we need to be sure everything is covered."

He rubbed the back of his neck. "I'm kind of busy."

"I understand, but this is a priority."

"I'm aware of that," he snapped. "But while you're free to do what you want, whenever you want, I have kids to think about."

The intensity of his words made her gasp. Was he deliberately trying to hurt her? To remind her of her loss. To emphasize that while tomorrow was Mother's Day, she'd be spending it alone, unable to hug her son or even talk to him on the telephone.

She narrowed her gaze on the perpetually grumpy man. Crockett knew exactly what he was doing. And here she thought their rocky relationship had turned a corner.

Without another word, she climbed into her SUV, eager to escape and wondering if it was too late to back out of the deal with the Renwicks. Because there was no way she and Crockett would ever be able to work together.

Crockett struggled to stay alert in church the next morning. He'd barely slept last night, and only in part because of Mac's injury. He should have gone to the festival. David had mentioned it, but Crockett had been determined to get the tack room cleared out and reorganized. He hated having to search for things.

Still, his kids were much more important. He should have been there for Mac when she needed him. He hadn't even been available when she'd called. What if it had been something worse and she'd had to go to the hospital?

Yet while that had played a role in his sleeplessness, it was the stricken look on Paisley's face that had haunted him all night. He'd behaved callously when he should have been thanking her profusely for looking after his daughter. Instead, he'd misdirected his frustration with himself and had taken it out on her.

He couldn't have been more cruel than he'd been in that moment, emphasizing the fact that he had kids and she didn't. What he'd said was downright mean. Now, as church dismissed, he had to find a way to make things right with Paisley, even if it might be easier to find a needle in a haystack.

Glancing across the aisle, he saw Mac sitting on the padded pew, giggling with her friends. Despite her foot feeling better, she'd insisted on using an old pair of crutches he'd had stashed in the closet, making her the center of attention.

"Dad." David patted his arm. "I left my Bible in Sunday school. I'll be right back."

"All right, buddy."

Alone, Crockett surveyed the rapidly emptying sanctuary until he spotted Paisley near the double doors at the back. She was talking with Rae, looking downright gorgeous in a pink floral sundress, her copper locks tumbling over her shoulders onto her back. The two friends hugged before going their separate ways, Rae continuing outside while Paisley went the opposite direction, bringing her right past him.

This is your chance.

He drew in a fortifying breath. "Paisley?"

Her steps slowed, and she lifted her chin, glancing his way without really looking at him. "Sorry, Crockett. I need to pick up something from the church office."

As she began to walk away, he said, "Would you care to join me and the kids for lunch?" When her retreat halted, he added, "It is Mother's Day, after all."

Her body went rigid as she turned her narrowed gaze on him. "And why would that matter, Crockett?" Her sugary drawl held a bite. "Because as you were so quick to point out, I don't have any children."

Chagrin washed over him in buckets. "Paisley, I—"

She held up a hand. "I will be contacting Mr. Hollings tomorrow morning."

"What for?"

"I'm withdrawing from our deal. Now if you'll excuse me." She turned on her high-heeled sandals and continued along the worn blue carpet.

Crockett watched her retreat, his insides knotting with regret. Paisley was giving up the very thing she'd so desperately wanted. And all because he'd taken his own failures out on her. He couldn't say that he blamed her. Yet, as the day wore on, the more his conscience prodded him like a hot poker. He had no idea how to right this ship, or if he even could, but he had to try and find a way to make amends.

After contacting a couple of the parents of Mac and David's friends, he dropped his kids off before continuing to Paisley's. He parked in front of the stately gray Victorian, his heart pounding as fat raindrops pelted the windshield. He should have apologized this morning. Instead, he'd asked her to lunch as if everything was hunky-dory. What kind of person does that?

Someone with major issues. Someone who'd been cast aside without so much as a second glance. Someone who found it easier to reject than be rejected.

He was that person. But Paisley didn't deserve his scorn.

Humidity enveloped him, threatening to steal his breath as he exited his truck. He stepped onto the sidewalk, pushed through the iron gate and marched onto the front porch. *God, whatever help You can give me here, I'd greatly appreciate it.*

He pressed the doorbell and waited. Several long moments later, Paisley opened the door. Dressed in black yoga pants and a flowing white tank top, she didn't appear very happy to see him.

"What is it, Crockett?"

Knowing he'd better say what he came to say before she slammed the door in his face, he mustered his courage. "I'm sorry, Paisley. For what I said to you last night. I was wrong. I treated you harshly when I should have been thanking you."

She clung to the door, wearily resting her head against it. "Why did you do that?"

"I was mad at myself for not being there for Mac."

"So, it made you feel better to throw verbal darts at me?" Hearing her say that made him feel even worse.

"I didn't mean to. It just…came out." He rubbed the back of his neck. "And in the process, I hurt you. I'm so sorry, Paisley. Truly I am."

Moving his hands to his hips, he stared at the

rain and hauled in a breath before meeting her sorrowful gaze once again. "Can you ever forgive me?"

Letting go of the door, she said, "Not unless you can answer one simple question."

"Fair enough."

"Why have you always treated me with such disdain?"

He blew out a breath. "I'm afraid that question is anything but simple." It would mean revealing a part of himself he preferred others didn't know about. He didn't want to be the object of anyone's pity.

Glancing through the screen, he said, "May I come in?"

After a lengthy pause, she pushed the screen door open and he stepped aside.

He followed her into the living room next to the entry hall, the sound of his boots on the wooden floor echoing off of the high ceiling. Paisley settled into one of two black-and-white-checked wingback chairs near the windows, eyeing the Atlanta Braves baseball game on the television that hung on the opposite wall, the sound muted.

His nerves were a jumbled mess as he eased onto the edge of the cream-colored sofa, trying to come up with the right words. "I…tend to be a rather guarded person."

Crossing her legs, she looked at him. "You don't say."

"My barriers go up when I'm around, well, women like you."

Her sapphire eyes narrowed slightly. "What do you mean 'like me'?"

"Beautiful. Driven to get what they want. Women who have an appreciation for life's finer things."

Now she just looked perplexed. "That's a backhanded compliment if I ever heard one. I wasn't aware those were bad traits."

"They can be." Standing, he paced to the front windows, knowing he was getting this all wrong. "Look, trust doesn't come easy for me. My mother and my ex-wife, Mac and David's mother, they both walked out of their children's lives. Out of my life."

Her eyes followed him back and forth. "So, first you treat me like dirt and then you lump me with two women who don't deserve to be called mothers?" Her brow furrowed as she watched him. "You're not doing yourself any favors, Crockett."

"I know." Again, he rubbed the back of his neck, wishing he was better with words.

"What do their actions have to do with the jab you threw at me last night?"

He dropped onto the sofa again, resting his

elbows on his knees as he stared at the pale gray area rug. "I wrongly assumed that you were faulting me for allowing Mac to go to the festival without supervision. Throwing the first punch was a defensive move, but I hit below the belt. You didn't deserve that." He forced himself to look at her. "Words can't express how sorry I am."

Paisley stared at her clasped hands. "First of all, Mackenzie is old enough to do some things alone with her friends. Second, I'm sorry your mother and your ex treated you with such disregard. But purposely hurting someone else because of what you *think* they might do." She looked at him now. "That makes you no better than them."

The reality of her words had him wishing the couch would swallow him up. There was no denying she was right. "I can assure you, I have no desire to be like either of them."

She nodded but remained silent.

If he only knew what was going through that mind of hers. Not that he could blame her for being upset.

"Paisley, I can't promise you that we won't be at odds with one another ever again, but I believe we have been given an opportunity to create something special. Something that will not only make people happy but, perhaps, benefit the people of Bliss. If you can somehow find it in your heart to forgive me for being the world's biggest jerk, I'd really like to see both of our dreams come true."

"For someone who was so skeptical, you sure have had a change of heart."

"What can I say? You won me over with your thoughtful insight on security measures."

"Don't you know anything about sales?" The corners of her mouth twitched. "You always try to overcome the buyer's objections."

He puffed out a laugh. "You're pretty smart, you know that?"

"And don't you ever forget it." She stood. "Thank you for being honest with me. I'm sure it wasn't easy. And I'm sorry the women in your life let you down. Just don't judge me by their actions."

"No, I don't think I'll be making that mistake again."

"Good." After a moment, she peered up at him. "We still need to create a single list of expectations and must-haves to present to the Renwicks."

He dared to hope. "Does that mean you forgive me?"

"It means I really want to see that castle restored."

For some inexplicable reason, his heart sank. If she couldn't forgive him—

"And yes, I forgive you."

Chapter Five

A squeal slipped from Paisley's lips as she pulled into Crockett's drive Wednesday evening. Not only had her kitchen window finally been replaced, Molly Renwick Simmons was coming to Bliss this weekend and wanted to meet with her and Crockett.

Paisley was thrilled that the woman was so eager to get things rolling at the castle when the contracts hadn't even been finalized. They'd arrived Tuesday and were now with a local attorney, but Molly said she had every confidence they'd work things out.

Yet, while the impromptu visit was a pleasant surprise, it left little time for Paisley and Crockett to take their individual ideas and combine them into one master plan they would then share with Molly. So as of eleven o'clock this morning, dinner at his place had been deemed a necessity.

Lord willing, it would be a productive evening, as opposed to ending in another disagreement.

Winding toward the house, her thoughts wandered to her conversation with Crockett on Sunday. No doubt, the women in his life had wounded him deeply, leaving painful scars on his heart. Paisley couldn't help wondering how old he'd been when his mother left. And to have his wife do the same to his children?

She shook her head, her heart aching for Mackenzie, David and the boy Crockett had once been. While she didn't appreciate the way Crockett had treated her, at least now she understood the motivations behind it. No one should feel unwanted.

After parking in the circle drive, she exited her SUV, armed with two pies. Since Crockett had offered to take care of the meal, the least she could do was provide dessert.

The front door opened before she reached the porch, and a smiling David appeared.

"Hi, Ms. Paisley!" His blue eyes sparkled with mirth as he approached.

"Hello there, David."

He eyed the two boxes in her hands. "What's in there?"

"Pies."

"What kind?" Hands buried in the pockets of his basketball shorts, he looked so hopeful.

"Lemon."

"Oh." His gaze fell as he toed the flagstone pavers with this high-top sneaker.

"And chocolate."

His head popped up. "I like chocolate."

"I know you do. That's why I made it." She lowered one hand. "Would you like to carry it for me?"

"Sure!" He carefully took hold with both hands before starting back into the house. "Dad's fixing dinner, and Mackenzie's setting the table."

The tangy aroma of tomato sauce and garlic teased Paisley's senses as she closed the door behind her and followed the boy through the living room to the kitchen.

"Hey, Ms. Paisley." Mackenzie waved with a fistful of silverware.

"Hi, darlin'."

Crockett turned from the stainless-steel stove to the long granite-topped island that distinguished the kitchen from the living space. "You're right on time. Lasagna is out of the oven, and the garlic bread just went in."

"Dad, Ms. Paisley brought us pie." David set his atop the creamy-gold countertop that coordinated beautifully with the rich maple cabinetry.

Paisley followed suit with hers, eyeing the way-too-handsome man opposite her. "Lemon or chocolate. What's your preference?"

Perching his hands on either side of the sink, he leaned forward, emphasizing his already large biceps. "You mean I can't have both?" The boyish look in his dark eyes had her cheeks warming.

"I believe that can be arranged. But only if you finish your dinner like a good boy."

He glanced toward the oven before sending her a mischievous grin. "I'm certain that won't be a problem."

"Dad, can I play my video game until dinner's ready?"

Crockett looked at his watch, then David. "You've got ten minutes, buddy."

"Cool." The boy took off across the living room and disappeared into a hallway.

Paisley's stomach growled as she savored the delightful aromas. "It smells divine in here."

"It's just Dad's 'specialty of the house.'" With the silverware all on the table, Mackenzie made air quotes with her fingers as she approached. "Frozen lasagna, frozen garlic bread and salad from a bag."

"Hey—" Crockett tossed a cup towel in his daughter's direction "—you're not supposed to reveal my chef secrets."

Mackenzie rolled her eyes and emphatically thrust the towel back in her father's direction. "Frozen food is not a secret."

"No, but it can be very good," said Paisley.

"See." Crockett grinned at the girl.

"Stop." Mackenzie hastily crossed her arms over her chest. "I'm still mad at you."

Her father sent her a warning look.

Though curious, Paisley wasn't about to pry.

"I wanted to have an end-of-school swim party." Mackenzie turned her attention to Paisley, seemingly eager to offer up the details. "But Daddy says I can't because it wouldn't be appropriate to host a bunch of girls with only a male for supervision."

"Mac..." Crockett glared at the girl.

It burned Paisley to no end that Mackenzie's mother had been so selfish as to abandon her children and put her daughter in such a position. If she were involved in their lives, she could at least help out in these sorts of situations. Instead, she'd robbed her children of some of life's simple pleasures.

Paisley palmed the girl's elbow. "I know you don't want to hear this, darlin', but your father's concerns are justified. Some parents might not be comfortable sending their daughters when there's not a female adult."

The girl lowered her head. "It's not fair."

Paisley agreed. It wasn't fair.

"I'm sorry, Mac." Crockett reached for a pot holder as the timer chimed on the stove. "That's just the way it is."

As he pulled the garlic bread from the oven, his daughter looked up, a glimmer of excitement brightening her brown eyes. "What if Ms. Paisley was here?" Her gaze shifted from her father to Paisley.

Unease rippled through Paisley. She did not want to get caught in the midst of an argument between father and daughter. What if Crockett didn't want to host a party and the absence of a female was simply an excuse? Then again, he was also the type to do anything for his children.

Setting the bubbling bread atop the stove, he said, "Mac, you can't just volunteer Paisley like that. It's not right."

While Paisley appreciated him stepping in for her, she really did want to help. She was all about parties, after all. But she couldn't very well make the offer without checking with Crockett first—and certainly not in front of his daughter.

Mackenzie glared at her father, then stormed out of the room in a huff.

Tossing the pot holders onto the counter, Crockett heaved out a sigh and shook his head. "She just doesn't get it."

"No, she doesn't." Paisley glanced to the hallway where the girl had disappeared. Looking back at Crockett, she said, "And I hate to be the bearer of bad news, but she's just getting started. She's still got her teen years ahead of her."

He cut her a sideways glance across the island. "Wow, thanks for the encouragement."

Biting back a smile, Paisley eased into one of three iron-backed barstools and clasped her hands atop the cool granite. "I didn't want to say anything in front of Mackenzie, but I'd be happy to help. That is, assuming you're willing to allow her to have a party."

"After the way she just behaved, I'm not sure she deserves it."

Paisley shrugged. "Your choice. But I'm happy to assist with planning, food and, of course, supervision."

His gaze narrowed. "That's an awful lot. I couldn't ask that of you."

"You didn't. I offered."

The corners of his mouth tilted upward. "I appreciate that. I don't think Mac grasps the fact that I want her to be able to have parties and sleepovers, all those things that other girls get to do. It's just that, in this day and age, and with me being a single dad, I worry how people will react."

"That is completely understandable. It's a shame, but your concerns are valid."

"Any idea how I should tell her? I mean, I can't just let her off the hook. Not after that little tantrum."

"You could tell her she has to help me with the planning and preparations."

His chuckle held a hint of sarcasm. "Are you kidding? She'd be all over that."

"Good point."

"I'll have to think on it. Right now, we have work to do and dinner is getting cold." He cupped his hands around his mouth. "Mac. David. Dinner." Turning back to the stove, he grabbed a knife and a cutting board and began slicing the aromatic bread.

"Anything I can do to help?" Paisley slid out of her chair.

"Salad is in the fridge, if you want to grab it."

Moving around the island, she reached for the door handle.

"It's in a bowl, not the bag," Crockett was quick to add.

Smiling, she opened the refrigerator. "Well, now I feel special." She retrieved the clear glass bowl filled with a mixture of romaine, carrots, red cabbage and tomatoes. As she set it on the table, Mackenzie entered the room. Instead of coming to the table, though, she tentatively moved into the kitchen, pausing beside her father.

With tears in her eyes and a pout on her lips, she looked up at him. "I'm sorry, Daddy. I shouldn't have gotten mad at you."

Setting the knife on the counter, he wrapped

his arms around his daughter and pulled her to him. "I love you, sweetness." He kissed the top of her head. "You know I'd do anything for you."

"I know." The girl sniffed.

The precious exchange had Paisley a little misty. Perhaps Mackenzie understood more than her father suspected. That knowledge made Paisley's heart ache all the more.

Crockett released his daughter. "You can have your swim party."

Taking a step back, Mackenzie wiped her tears with the heels of her hands. "But you said—"

"Paisley has offered to help."

The girl's gaze shifted to Paisley as a wide smile graced her beautiful face. "Really?"

She nodded. "Whatever you need, darlin'."

Mackenzie charged toward her, practically bowling her over with the force of her hug. "Thank you, thank you, thank you."

"You're welcome." Paisley smoothed a hand over the girl's silky hair, savoring the embrace. Her newfound awareness of Mackenzie and David's situation had her longing to help them any way she could. But first she'd have to prove herself worthy of Crockett's trust. Given how he had been let down, that might be an uphill battle.

Papaw's dream was finally coming true.

Rain peppered Crockett's windshield as he

pulled up to Renwick Castle Saturday morning. Despite the gray skies, he was on top of the world. Mac was going to get her swim party, he and Paisley had synced their lists with few disagreements and, as of yesterday, the contracts on the castle had been approved, signed and were now on their way back to the Renwicks' attorney.

Crockett and Paisley were officially employees of the Renwicks for a term of ten years, with options to extend. In addition to managerial salaries, they would maintain exclusive rights to the castle's use and profit-share with the Renwicks.

Now, he was about to meet with the castle's owner and begin the process of sharing his passion for Texas history with others. Thankfully, the college-age girl who was going to be nannying the kids this summer was already home from school and able to stay with them today.

Eyeing the luxury rental car parked near the front door, he tried to remember when the notion of a museum had become important to him. His grandfather had talked about it for so long that Crockett had a hard time figuring out where Papaw's desires left off and his began. Still, as the decades passed, it had been little more than a pipe dream…until the day Crockett realized he had the means to make his grandfather's vision a reality.

Granted, things had turned out different than

he'd imagined. Still, he wished his grandfather could be here to share in the adventure.

Movement in his periphery had him twisting to see Paisley's SUV turning into the drive. He grabbed his notebook and umbrella and exited his truck.

Opening the umbrella, he continued toward Paisley as her door opened. "You ready?"

Her smile was wide as she stepped out, closing her door before slipping under the umbrella. Hair pulled up into one of those perfectly messy updos, she looked fashionable yet professional in skinny jeans and a white shirt topped with a navy blazer. "Are you kidding? This is the equivalent of Christmas morning to a seven-year-old. I barely slept last night."

"I know what you mean." He'd done a fair amount of tossing and turning himself.

The front door swung open before they reached the stoop, and a woman with straight, shoulder-length, salt-and-pepper hair stepped under the stone portico. Her gray slacks and a tailored white button-down shirt seemed rather stuffy, though she smiled politely as they approached.

"Mr. Devereaux and Ms. Wainwright, I presume."

"Yes, ma'am." Crockett closed the umbrella as they stepped under the portico.

"It's a pleasure to meet you, Mrs. Simmons." Paisley extended her hand.

"Oh, please—" the woman waved off the comment and took hold "—call me Molly." Moments later, she turned her attention to Crockett.

He, too, offered his hand, only to have it enfolded in both of hers. "You can call me Crockett."

"That's a very Texas-sounding name, young man." The woman, who was probably only a few years older than him and stood almost a foot shorter than his six foot three, peered up at him through quirky red-framed glasses.

"Thank you. I'm kind of partial to it." He left the umbrella outside as they moved into the entry hall.

"On behalf of my cousin and myself, I want to thank the two of you for contacting us about the castle." Molly closed the door behind them. "Quite honestly, we'd both forgotten about the place. Neither of us really spent any time here as children, so any memories we had are long-forgotten."

"That's a shame." Paisley paused beside the knight's armor. "I would think visiting a castle would be a wonderful opportunity to spark a child's imagination."

Crockett could certainly attest to that. His imagination had run wild in this place.

"Perhaps. But with the company headquartered in the northeast and Bliss being rather out of the way, it wasn't practical. Of course, neither Jared's nor my father had much interest in the old castle. To them, it was simply the frivolity of an old Scotsman."

Having met Molly's grandfather when he was a boy, Crockett was pretty sure Charles hadn't viewed his grandfather's legacy as something frivolous.

Curious, Crockett studied the woman. "How do *you* feel about the castle?"

"I think you were absolutely correct when you referred to it as a 'unique piece of Texas history,' one that shouldn't be left to ruin. Your ideas of using it as a museum and for weddings and other events are absolutely stellar. However, we have much work to do to get to that point, so let's get started."

Molly strode deeper into the entry hall. "We know the infrastructure will need to be inspected and, perhaps, overhauled. Things like electricity, plumbing, air-conditioning." She paused, fanning herself. "Is it always so humid here?"

"Welcome to the coastal plains of Texas," said Crockett. "Where we tend to get a lot of moisture from the Gulf."

Paisley's gaze moved from him to Molly. "However, we are experiencing a wetter-than-normal spring, so things are a little damper than usual."

"Judging by the jungle outside, I should say so." Molly tugged at the hem of her shirt. "Now, where was I? Ah, yes. Infrastructure. We should also have the house inspected to make sure everything is structurally sound." She planted a fist on one hip. "Have you seen the kitchen?"

"Yes," Crockett and Paisley said in unison.

"Good, then you're aware that it needs to be gutted and updated."

"It should also be a commercial kitchen." Paisley looked from her notes to Molly.

"Indeed," said Molly. "Nothing but stainless steel."

Paisley grinned.

"Let's go upstairs." Molly started toward the grand staircase.

Crockett hesitated. "Are you aware of the stairs in the northeast tower?" Perhaps that might jog Molly's memory.

Her hand on the railing, Molly paused. "I'd forgotten all about them." Her smile seemed to indicate he'd achieved his goal. "Let's use those." Doing an about-face, she continued toward the back of the castle and made a left turn.

An elbow nudge had him turning to see Paisley's thumbs-up as they followed, only to halt soon after when Molly abruptly stopped at the base of the tower.

"What is this mark?" She pointed to a dark streak in the stone approximately twenty inches above the floor. "I vaguely remember it being there when I was a child, though I must have been too busy playing to ask about it."

"That's from the 1913 flood." Crockett looked from Molly to Paisley. "Heavy rains caused the river to come out of its banks. More than half of the town was cut off by floodwaters. Someone marked the water level for posterity."

"Has it flooded since?" Paisley's eyes were wide.

"Not that I'm aware of." He shrugged. "Or else no one bothered to mark it. It's just another fascinating bit of the castle's history."

"Indeed." Molly started up the staircase.

"What compelled Angus Renwick to build a castle?" Paisley eyed Molly as they moved into the ballroom a short time later.

"From what I was told, he wanted to bring a little bit of Scotland to his new home. This wasn't his primary residence, though."

"Oh?" Paisley looked surprised.

"Angus was a cattle baron." Crockett smiled at Molly. "He had a few thousand acres out west of town."

"Land that has long since left the family," Molly was quick to add.

"Ah, but it's where he built his fortune." Crockett moved deeper into the ballroom. "He hosted parties and such at the castle. It even served briefly as a hospital."

"Really?" Paisley's sapphire eyes went wide, obviously intrigued by the revelation.

"During a yellow fever epidemic," Crockett continued. "The town had no hospital and the castle had plenty of room."

"That's when Angus met my great-great-grandmother." Molly beamed. "The poor man had left Scotland with a broken heart and a promise that he would never love again. Then he met Mary, a nurse twenty years his junior. Six months later they were married."

"Oh, I love that." Paisley pressed a hand to her chest.

"It is a rather romantic story," Molly mused. "One that shows just how powerful love can be."

"Yes, and now I really can't wait to start having weddings here."

On the third floor Molly deemed that the atrocious carpet had to go, and they all agreed that the original long leaf pine floors should be refinished. Then it was determined that the bedrooms could be used for bridal parties and, perhaps, conference rooms.

By the time they returned to the first level, Crockett could hardly wait to get started.

Standing in the entry hall again, Molly said, "The thing that bothers me most about this place is that it's so dark. I know we're not able to add more windows, but I believe we could brighten things up a bit by either removing all of this dark wood on the walls and ceiling or, perhaps, covering it with a bright white paint."

Crockett felt his eyes widen as he and Paisley exchanged a look. "With all due respect—" he shifted his attention to Molly "—the woodwork is integral to the character of the castle. Not only is it made of ancient mahogany, it adds warmth to all of the stone and makes it reminiscent of the Scottish castles Angus grew up around."

"Yes," Paisley continued, "the old-world look is what will appeal to visitors, evoking thoughts of medieval knights, princes and fairy tales. It's what makes Renwick Castle unique—and unique is what sells."

One arm across her midsection, Molly perched her other elbow atop it and settled her chin between her thumb and forefinger as she scrutinized the space.

Unwilling to let things go, Crockett forged on. "Angus modeled Renwick castle after real places he visited as a young man. Everything from the location to the gardens to the interior brought back fond memories for him. We don't want to erase those memories. However, we could brighten things up with lighting. Even the smallest, most unobtrusive LED lights can change things considerably."

After a long moment, Molly said, "I suppose this means you want to keep that thing, then." She pointed to the knight's armor near the entrance.

Paisley smiled. "It definitely sets the stage."

Molly cocked her head. "In a kitschy sort of way." Another moment ticked by as she continued to ponder. "I suppose that, since the castle is going to be a destination as opposed to a home, unique would be the best approach." She lowered her arms. "All right, you've talked me into it."

Crockett released the breath he'd been holding. "Thank you, Molly. I promise, you won't be disappointed."

"No, I don't believe I will. I trust the two of you to do the right thing. Between your knowledge of the castle's history and Paisley's sense of style, I think you two were the right choice. You'll be terrific partners. I mean, just look at how you teamed together just now to convince me."

Him and Paisley partners. Who'd have thought?

That is, assuming he didn't mess things up again.

Chapter Six

Since Molly had given Paisley and Crockett keys to the castle, stating they could begin work whenever they liked, Paisley woke Monday morning, ready to hit the ground running.

After delivering chocolate chunk cookies, gingersnaps and scotcharoos to Rae's and grabbing her daily cappuccino, she went to Bliss Hardware to get some moving boxes. Per Molly's request, what remained of the castle's contents, save for the knight's armor and the majority of the kitchen items, would be picked up by movers in a few weeks and sent to the Renwicks. Still, Paisley wanted to get a head start by boxing up some of the smaller items. Anything that would make her feel as though they were making progress.

She wasn't keen on the idea of working without the benefit of air-conditioning, but until they were able to get things inspected, she'd simply have to deal with the heat and humidity. After all, she wasn't about to waste precious time, not when she hoped to have the castle open for business before the holidays. That gave her a good five months. Since they weren't doing anything structural, it was definitely doable.

After parking, she headed into the hardware store where she found Christa, the store's owner, behind the cash register.

"And how's my favorite newlywed?" Paisley hugged her friend as she rounded the counter.

"Just peachy."

"And Sadie?" After the death of his sister and brother-in-law, Christa's husband, Mick, became guardian for his six-year-old niece.

"Ready for school to be out," said Christa.

"She's in kindergarten. How bad can it be?"

"I know, right?" She skimmed her chin-length brown hair behind her ear. "I think it's the riding lessons we promised that's got her so excited. She loves horses."

Crockett's training facility came to mind. "Where is she taking lessons?"

"Kacey Garrett, the ag teacher at the high school, teaches little buckaroo classes out at her place during the summer."

"Kacey's a sweetheart. Sadie's going to love her." Paisley noticed the plastic sheeting that covered an opening on the far wall. "How's the store expansion coming?"

"Good. Another month or so and our new home design center should be open." Christa elbowed her as they strolled away from the checkout counter, a glimmer in her hazel eyes. "So what have you been up to? Laurel said you got the castle and you're going to be working with Crockett Devereaux." Her voice held an incredulous tone. "Whose idea was that? Last time I checked, you two were perpetually at odds with each other."

"Pretty much." Paisley explained the Renwicks' offer. "It was an all-or-nothing deal, but one that was important enough for us to set aside our differences."

"If you say so. I just hope you don't kill each other in the process."

"Oh, it's not that bad." She swatted her friend, knowing that she and Crockett had come a long way these past couple of weeks. "And now that we've officially been given the go-ahead, I need some packing boxes and tape, please."

"Sounds like you're not wasting any time."

She followed Christa toward the back of the store. "I can't afford to, not if I want the work completed before the holidays."

Her friend paused. "What about the B and B?"

"I expect I'll be far too busy to host any guests for a while."

A short time later, Paisley's SUV was filled with every box Bliss Hardware had in stock. She drove across town, grateful for the bright morning sun. With no electricity to illuminate the castle, the sun was her friend, even if it did up the temperature. She prayed Crockett could get those inspectors out there soon.

Pulling up to the castle, she worked through the half a dozen or so keys Molly had given her until she found the one to unlock the gate. She parked near the entrance, then grabbed her leather tote, cappuccino and insulated water cup and stepped outside.

Her shorts-and-tank-top-clad body vibrated with energy as she made her way onto the covered porch and unlocked the door. Her dream had come true. Part of it, anyway. And soon, she'd be bringing fairy-tale weddings to life.

Once inside the musty space, she decided on a quick walk-through before getting started. With Crockett at the gravel plant this morning, she had the perfect opportunity to familiarize herself with the intricacies of the castle. Though, with no one else there, the place was eerily quiet, and every little sound had her twisting to look for its source. At this rate, she'd have whiplash by lunchtime.

Once she had made her way upstairs, she strolled around the ballroom, smiling as she envisioned brides and grooms dancing beneath sparkling chandeliers. How many times had Angus and Mary Renwick waltzed in here? Paisley had been thinking about the couple ever since Crockett and Molly shared those historical nuggets with her. Learning that a brokenhearted Angus had found love again spoke to the romantic in Paisley and gave her hope that, perhaps, one day she might find love again, too.

Then again, she'd never be able to duplicate what she and Peter had. They were a perfect match. Saying goodbye had been excruciatingly painful, and if she had to go through that again…

No, she wasn't going to go there.

With a parting glance, she left the ballroom and moved downstairs, making a mental note to pick Crockett's brain for more of the castle's history. He sure knew a lot about this place—maybe even more than Molly did—and that information could be helpful for marketing.

On the main level, she headed to the library, grabbed a roll of packing tape and assembled several boxes. Floor-to-ceiling shelves covered the walls on either side of the fireplace, all laden with novels from a bygone era. At least they were easy to pack, so it shouldn't take her long. Yet an hour later, she'd barely made a dent. There were far more books than she'd initially thought—so many that she began inventorying them on her phone so she could make Molly aware of what all was there.

With the aid of the flashlight on her phone, she realized there wasn't a single volume less than fifty years old and most were much older than that, including first edition copies of *The Adventures of Tom Sawyer*, *Twenty Thousand Leagues Under the Sea* and *Little Women*, among other classics.

When her stomach growled around one thirty, she was more than ready for a break. How could something so simple become so painstaking? She retrieved the ham and cheese sandwich she'd packed in her tote, along with a bag of carrots and a packet of wipes.

After cleaning her dust-covered hands, she pulled her sandwich from the plastic bag, perched on a gold-and-green wingback chair near the fireplace and mindlessly stared at the carved wooden mantel as she ate. Despite the dim lighting and decades of soot buildup, she soon noticed something more than just a random design. Was that a longhorn?

She stood, excitement coursing through her as she pulled her phone from the back pocket of her shorts and turned on the flashlight.

"This is exquisite." The carving on the front of

the mantel was of a cattle drive. Complete with longhorns, cowboys and horses.

Stepping back, she tried to take in the image as a whole, but there just wasn't enough light to do it justice. She turned, eyeing the heavy gold brocade curtains. Even though they were open, they still blocked a portion of each of the two smaller windows on either side of a larger one.

She examined the rods that were near the top of the twelve-foot wall. If she had a ladder, she could take those down. She'd have to run home and grab hers.

Still nibbling on her sandwich, she wandered into the entry hall, wondering if there was a ladder around here somewhere. After all, people had once called the castle home. She'd been all through the house, though, and hadn't seen one. Still…

Maybe in the kitchen.

Sandwich gone, she dusted off her hands and headed that way, praying she wouldn't run into any little critters along the way. Pushing through the swinging door, she noticed it was even darker in there. From now on, she needed to bring a flashlight because her phone wasn't cutting it.

No signs of a ladder, however there was a door that led outside. Paisley could see a small outbuilding through the window. Problem was, getting there involved walking through a lot of tall weeds and grass. A perfect hiding place for snakes.

Good thing she'd thrown her rubber boots into her SUV this morning.

She quickly retrieved them and changed out of her slip-on sneakers before cautiously picking her way through knee-high grass to the old wooden shed with peeling white paint. *Lord, please don't let there be anything unsavory in there.*

Reaching for the door, she noticed the padlock barring her entry. She could only hope one of the keys Molly gave her would open it. Fortunately, they were still in her pocket.

On her third try, the lock popped open. And right inside the door was a wooden six-foot ladder. Despite its weight, she lugged it back to the house and into the library, grateful for the lightweight aluminum ladders they made today.

The trio of windows had been dressed as one, and longer rods were always more difficult to maneuver. But she was nothing if not determined. And tomorrow when she came, she was going to bring window cleaning supplies.

She climbed the ladder, quickly realizing just how high twelve-foot ceilings really were. Even at five foot ten, she had to go all the way to the last rung before she could reach the rod. She attempted to lift it, but it wouldn't budge. It looked as though it was made of brass. Real brass, not the brass finish they sell nowadays. But why wouldn't it lift out?

Further inspection revealed that the pole didn't simply rest in the brackets, it went through the brackets, making this a two-person job.

"Well, boo." In her attempt to straighten, she lost her balance.

The ladder wobbled beneath her, causing her to sway even more.

She grabbed hold of the curtain rod in an effort to stabilize herself. But her still-booted foot slipped, sending the ladder toppling away from her.

A scream caught in her throat as she latched on to the pole with her other hand. Moments later, she found herself dangling as the racket beneath her finally ceased.

Her breaths were fast and furious. How was she going to get down?

Fortunately, the pole was sturdy. Her grip, on the other hand, was growing sweatier by the second.

This was such a bad idea. Almost as bad as letting go. She didn't relish the thought of breaking a bone.

She studied the window in front of her. It was narrow enough that she might be able to stretch her legs and arms between the casings and walk herself down the way Logan had done in one of the doorways at their house outside of Atlanta. Until she scolded him, anyway. Now she just needed to figure out how he'd done it.

She shoved her left foot against the far casing then finagled the right into place. Sort of. Talk about awkward. But desperate times called for desperate measures. Now, if she could just duck under the upper casing.

A sound echoed from the entry hall.

"Paisley?" She couldn't decide if Crockett's timing was good or bad.

"In here." She hated the panic in her voice.

She heard his footfalls until—

"What on earth?" He rushed toward her, clamped his hands around her waist and eased her to the floor.

"Oh, thank you." The breathless words spilled from her lips as she turned and dropped her forehead against him. "That was terrifying."

"What were you doing up there?"

"I needed more light, so I was attempting to take the curtains down and accidentally knocked the ladder over." Her breathing leveling off, she looked up to discover deep caramel eyes filled with concern fixed on her. She swallowed, once, twice, wondering when and how her hands had come to rest against Crockett's muscular chest.

Beneath her fingertips his heart pounded almost as erratically as her own.

"Good thing I showed up when I did." A mischievous smile played at his lips. "I only wish I'd had time to get a picture of you up there straddled between that window."

"Crockett Devereaux." Frowning, she lowered her hands and pushed out of his embrace, away from the appealing scent of sunshine and hard work, and turned so he couldn't see the heat in her cheeks. "You are a brat." A brat who swept in right when she needed him, reminding her how good it felt to have a protector.

She rubbed her arms, struggling to recall how long it had been since a man had held her. Obviously, too long if she was reacting so strongly to the one that only two weeks ago she'd considered her arch enemy. And while they'd become more amicable in recent days, there certainly wasn't anything romantic between them, nor would there ever be.

Glancing over her shoulder, she watched Crockett right the ladder. He was a wounded soul with trust issues. Yet trust was the basis for any good relationship, so she'd best get ahold of her ridiculous thoughts and concentrate on the castle. After all, there would never be anything more than business between her and Crockett.

* * *

After dropping the kids at school Wednesday morning, Crockett continued on to the castle and parked outside its walls, afraid to attempt maneuvering the gooseneck trailer he'd used to haul his tractor and shredder through the castle gates. One wrong move and he'd be taking a crash course in stone repair.

He took a swig of coffee from his travel mug and looked up at the pale gray sky, thankful the safety inspectors had chosen yesterday to visit Devereaux Sand and Gravel. Though definitely not his favorite part of running a business, it had given him an excuse not to be at the castle with Paisley. After what happened Monday afternoon, the last thing he wanted to do was share the same space as her.

How could she smell so good after working in that musty house all morning? Like vanilla and spice. Warm. Inviting. Comforting. Much like the woman herself.

Dropping his skull against the headrest, he scrubbed a hand over his face. What was wrong with him? So he hadn't been in that close proximity to a woman since Shannon walked out his door five years ago. That didn't mean Paisley should have had that kind of effect on him. She was a friend and business partner and nothing more.

The morning air was still and sticky as he got out of his truck to unlock the castle gates before moving to the trailer. Tackling the unruly castle grounds was his top priority today. And with four acres of tall grass to tend to, the shredder was his best option for bringing it under control. Once the grass was at a manageable height he'd come back with the zero-turn mover for the actual grooming process. He didn't know how long it would take him to return the grounds to the way they'd looked when his grandfather cared for the place, but he was determined to do his best. Besides, working outside would keep him away from Paisley.

He removed the tie-downs from the eight-foot aluminum ladder he'd brought from home. Paisley had risked life and limb in an attempt to take down those curtains Monday. The least he could do was see to it they were removed without issue.

The sound of an engine had him looking up as Paisley's SUV eased alongside him.

"Wow." She eyed his John Deere. "You brought out the big guns."

"Quickest way to get rid of all that high grass."

"I expect so."

"Gate's already open, so you can go on in." He hoisted the ladder off of the trailer and followed her.

She stepped out of her vehicle as he approached,

wearing a gray Georgia Bulldogs shirt over denim shorts.

Knowing what a staunch fan she was, he said, "You know, you could get into trouble wearing a shirt like that around these parts."

"Not likely." In the shade of a large live oak in need of some pruning, she tossed the door closed. "This Bulldog isn't intimidated by Longhorns or Aggies." She pointed at his Texas A&M shirt.

"I see. Just ladders, huh?" He gestured to the one he held.

Crossing her arms over her chest, she narrowed her gaze, seemingly pondering her retort. "Does this mean you're planning to help me with the curtains?"

"Maybe. If you ask me nicely."

Her arms promptly dropped, and she continued to the back of her SUV. "Now that I've cleaned the windows in the library, they're just fine where they are."

He puffed out a laugh, recalling her annoyance with him the other day. "Now who's behaving like a brat?"

"That reminds me." She sashayed toward him, years of dried leaves crunching beneath her sneakered feet. "The church committee meeting last night."

"What about it?"

"The vote was unanimous for the sand-colored carpet."

"I'm aware. I was there, remember?"

"That means you voted against your idea for the wood-look tile."

He sure had. With good reason. "I was coerced."

One perfectly arched brow lifted in question.

"A couple of the more mature ladies in the congregation cornered me after church Sunday. They let me know in no uncertain terms that they did not approve of my idea."

"Imagine that." She smirked. "Though I'm surprised someone as prickly as you allowed them to intimidate you."

His own gaze inadvertently narrowed. Paisley thought he was prickly? "Trust me, they might come across as sweet little old ladies, but they can make life difficult for anyone who crosses them, and I have Mac and David to think about."

"I see. Well, perhaps you should have thought of them before you brought up the idea, instead of looking for ways to stick it to me." That jab was as unexpected as a left hook.

First she called him prickly and now she was calling him out for something that happened weeks ago? He thought they were making a fresh start. Obviously, he was wrong. But then, when women were involved, he always got things wrong.

"I'll put this inside, just in case." Without another word, he fished his set of keys out of his pocket and deposited the ladder in the entry hall before returning to his truck. He wasn't sure what bugged him more. That Paisley called him out or that it bothered him. All he knew was that he was glad he didn't have to be anywhere near her anytime soon.

Pausing at the truck, he donned his protective glasses and noise-reducing earmuffs before climbing atop the tractor to ease it off the trailer. He maneuvered it up the castle drive and onto the grass. The shredder cut a wide swath as he slowly moved beyond the castle and toward the river, the aroma of fresh-cut grass filling the air. All the while, Crockett tried to figure out why Paisley's words had stung so much.

Maybe because she's right.

Yes, he had challenged her from time to time, but he'd told her why. Obviously, it hadn't changed her opinion of him. That is, unless she wasn't who she appeared to be.

He continued along the riverbank, eyeing the fast-moving water. Now that Paisley had gotten what she wanted—the castle—she had no need to stay on his good side. What if everything she'd done prior to signing those contracts and meeting with Molly was simply to get him to go along?

Do you really think she was faking it when she protected your children during the storm?

She'd protected herself, too. Besides, his kids were his weak spot. What if she was using them to get into his good graces?

A breeze sifted over him as he turned the tractor onto the far edge of the property, his stomach knotting. Paisley was supposed to help Mac with her party this Saturday. At least that was what she'd promised before their meeting with Molly. What if she conveniently had a change in plans?

Mac had always thought a lot of Paisley.

True, but Paisley wasn't making her promises before. His daughter had heard enough lies from her mother. Crockett wasn't about to see Mac hurt again.

By the time he traded the tractor for his pole-saw to trim several low-hanging limbs a few hours later, he was regretting having ever consented to the Renwicks' offer. If they hadn't been willing to sell the castle, then he should have just left it alone and gone on down the road. Instead he'd allowed himself to be sucked in by memories and false promises.

You're forgetting that Paisley was ready to back out, but you talked her out of it.

Big mistake on his part.

He was in the process of trimming the pecan tree he and Papaw used to gather nuts from when he noticed movement in his periphery. A quick glance revealed Paisley moving toward him with an insulated bag dangling from one arm. She stopped a few feet away, obviously wanting his attention.

Reluctantly, he killed the engine on the saw and removed his hearing protection. "Yes?"

Her gaze slipped from his to scan the freshly mown grounds and the river. "It looks great out here. You did a good job. The tractor was a smart idea."

Why was she suddenly being so nice?

"Thanks."

"That's a big pecan tree." She slipped the bag from her arm to hold it with both hands.

Birds chirped overhead as he swiped an arm across his brow, thinking how nice some water would be right now. "What's in the bag?"

"A peace offering." After a slight hesitation, she looked him in the eye. "For what I said about you trying to stick it to me. I was out of line. Guess I got a little caught up in my gloating. I'm sorry. You apologized to me, and I forgave you. I had no business resurrecting past sins."

Crockett was at a loss for words. He wasn't expecting an apology. On the contrary, he was ready to dig in and go to battle.

Because you keep comparing Paisley to Shannon instead of seeing her for who she is.

Old hurts were hard to put away. Particularly when his children were involved.

"I, uh…" He rubbed the back of his neck, not knowing what to say. "What does this peace offering look like?"

She smiled then. "Lunch. Chicken salad sandwiches, chips and peach cobbler."

A nervous laugh spilled out. "Have I mentioned how much I love peach cobbler?"

"Would you hold it against me if I say yes so you'll think I made it especially for you?"

"No, but God kind of frowns on that whole lying thing."

"True. Which is why I try to avoid it."

"Who needs the guilt, right?"

"Right." Head lowered, she looked at him through long lashes. "Will you join me for lunch, then?"

Thinking about the temper tantrum he'd been having all morning, he felt rather childish. Paisley wasn't afraid to own up to her mistakes, which was a new concept to him. She wasn't like Shannon. Perhaps one day he'd come to realize that.

"These clouds have kept the heat down today. Would you like to eat on the terrace?"

Shoulders relaxing, she smiled. "I think that

sounds delightful. And maybe you can help me come up with some menu ideas for Mackenzie's party."

"I can do that." Food wasn't a problem for him. However, an entire evening with Paisley could prove he'd bitten off more than he could chew.

Chapter Seven

Paisley asked Crockett to drop Mackenzie off at her house after school on Friday so they could start preparing for Saturday's party. First on the agenda was a trip to the dollar store for some party favors, decorations and tableware. Then they stopped by the grocery store so Mackenzie could pick out her favorite chips, ice cream and sprinkles before heading back to Paisley's to start cooking.

After much thought, not to mention input from Crockett, David and Mackenzie's friends, they'd decided on a menu of hamburger sliders so Crockett could show off his grilling prowess, pizza pinwheels, Paisley's famous fried mac and cheese balls, chips, carrot sticks and fruit. Or as Paisley liked to call it, a grab-and-go menu. Dessert was handled in a similar fashion, with the exception of the ice cream. But cupcakes and chocolate-covered pretzel rods were always a hit.

"What should we make first?" Mackenzie set the bag from the dollar store on the table.

Stowing the cookies and cream, vanilla and chocolate ice cream in the freezer, Paisley thought for a moment. "Since the macaroni and cheese will have to cook and cool before it can be made into balls, we'll start with that. Once it's in the refrigerator, we'll start on the cupcakes and pretzels."

"Okay." Crockett's daughter moved to the island. "What do you want me to do?"

Paisley closed the freezer. "How about you grate the cheese while I start cooking the macaroni?"

The girl smiled. "Sure."

After supplying Mackenzie with a cutting board, a grater and the cheese, Paisley put the water on to boil.

"It's so cool that you and my dad are working on the castle. I can't wait to see it."

"Perhaps, now that school is out, your dad can bring you and David by one day."

"Really?"

"Of course. So long as your father doesn't mind."

"Maybe Ashley could bring us." Mackenzie

was a third of the way through the block of sharp cheddar. "She'd probably like to see it, too."

"Who's Ashley?" And why did the thought of Crockett having a girlfriend bother Paisley?

"Our nanny. She's home from college for the summer. She's cool."

"Good. I'm glad you like her." Though the sense of relief flooding through Paisley was enough to make her cringe. "Will you still be working in the training barn?"

"Yeah." Mackenzie fell quiet for a long moment. "Did you mean what you said about us going shopping in the city?"

"Of course I did. However, you'll need to save some money first."

"I know. Maybe I can even do some extra chores to earn more."

Obviously, the trip meant more to Mackenzie than Paisley anticipated.

Two hours later, the macaroni and cheese was in the refrigerator and the cupcakes were frosted. All they had left to do was dip the pretzel rods. An easy task, though it took some time.

Paisley melted the white chocolate in the microwave then stirred it until it was smooth.

"Want to know my secrets for getting just the right amount of coating on the pretzels?"

Excitement flickered in Mackenzie's dark eyes. "Yes, please."

"First, I put the chocolate into one of these." Paisley held up a slender vase that was almost as tall as the pretzels were long. The sweet scent of vanilla wafted into the air as she poured the white liquid into the container. "Then I place the vase into a glass of hot water to keep the chocolate warm, so it won't solidify as quickly."

The girl watched as though taking it all in. "Good idea."

"Thank you. I thought it was rather clever." She picked up a pretzel. "Now we dip the pretzel rod into the chocolate." Or white chocolate in this case. "Leaving an inch or two as the base so we won't get chocolate all over our fingers when we're eating it."

Mackenzie giggled.

"Here's another one of my secrets." Paisley grabbed a silicone scraper. "When I pull the pretzel out, I gently tap the bare end of the pretzel, sending the excess chocolate back into the vase." She tapped it a few times. "Have you got the sprinkles ready?"

"Yes, ma'am." Mackenzie held up the plastic container of rainbow sprinkles.

"All right. I'll hold the dipped pretzel over this baking sheet while you add the sprinkles, that way we won't have sprinkles all over the floor." While Paisley twisted and turned the pretzel, Makenzie dropped the colorful candies.

"Do you think that's enough?"

"That's your call, Mackenzie. There's no right or wrong here. If it looks good to you, we'll call it good."

"Maybe just a little more."

"Go for it."

Two shakes later, Paisley said, "Now we'll set the coated pretzel over here on this parchment paper to dry." She laid it to one side. "And that's it. Would you like to do the next one?"

"Can I?"

"Of course."

"Can I use the milk chocolate?"

"You may."

Forty-five minutes later, the last pretzel was covered.

Mackenzie set it alongside the others, her eyes sparkling with pride. "They're so pretty."

Pretzels covered in rainbow, pink and blue sprinkles stretched across the island.

"Yes, they are. You have a very good eye for color."

"Thank you for letting me help. I learned a lot. My mom never liked to do stuff like this. She usually just bought stuff that was already made."

"That's all right." Paisley moved the dirty dishes to the sink and rinsed her hands. "Some people don't like to cook." Wiping her hands, she turned to see Mackenzie's smile falter.

"My mom didn't do much with me. Even when she and Dad were together, she was always gone."

Paisley couldn't imagine a mother not wanting to spend time with her children. "Sometimes adults get busy."

The girl lifted a shoulder. "I don't think she liked us very much. She really didn't like my dad. She always yelled at him."

For the second time today, Paisley cringed. Mackenzie's belief that her mother didn't like her broke Paisley's heart, and the fact that Mackenzie picked up on her mother's dislike of Crockett spoke volumes.

Paisley set the towel aside. "Do you ever see your mom?"

"It's been a long time." The girl met her gaze. "She used to call and promise that we would go and do stuff together, but she'd always cancel."

"How come?"

"I don't know. She just always said she couldn't."

Paisley's fists balled at her sides. She would give anything to be able to see Logan again. So how Mackenzie and David's mother could treat her children with such disregard was incomprehensible. To think that someone could be so selfish was downright sickening. Mackenzie and David deserved better. They deserved to know their mother loved them without condition. That she was someone they could count on to be there no matter what. That she had their backs. That she wanted them.

A knock sounded at the door.

Her gaze darted across the room to see Crockett and David on the porch.

Mackenzie hurried around the island to let them in. "Come see what we made."

Crockett's gaze collided with Paisley's the moment he walked in and remained there longer than usual. "They're gorgeous," he said as Mackenzie showed him the cupcakes and pretzels, though his gaze seemed riveted to Paisley's.

"Um…" Paisley tucked a lock of hair behind her ear, trying to pretend she didn't feel the intensity of Crockett's stare. "There are plenty, so you're welcome to have one." She dared a glance at the man. "Excuse me, please." She darted through the entry hall and onto the front porch where she gasped for air. The sense of protectiveness she felt for Mackenzie and David was overwhelming, and she had to remind herself that they weren't her children. So how could she take such offense to their mother's actions?

"Paisley?" Crockett pushed through the screen door, closing the main door behind him. "Are you all right?"

"I'm fine."

"You don't look fine. Did Mackenzie do something to upset you?"

She whirled to face him. "How could you

think such a thing? Of course she didn't. She's as sweet as the day is long. It's just…" A guttural growl escaped before she could stop it.

"Okay." Crockett took a step back. "Something's got you in a tizzy, though. Care to tell me about it?"

"No." She wouldn't break Mackenzie's confidence. "However, I will tell you this. You have been given two beautiful, amazingly wonderful children. Gifts from God that should be cherished beyond measure."

Hands clasped, he looked the epitome of calm while her insides were flailing like a rag doll. "You'll get no argument from me."

His words stopped her cold. She looked into his dark eyes that were so like Mackenzie's. He was a good father, one who put his children's needs above his own. One who was doing his best to see to it that Mackenzie and David had the best life possible despite their mother's betrayal. Something Paisley would do well to remember.

She sucked in a long breath and willed herself to calm down. "Good. As long as you're aware."

One thing was for certain, though. She would take Mackenzie shopping in the city. And Paisley would make certain she knew just how important she was.

The following afternoon, Crockett stood at the wall of windows that overlooked the pool at his place, watching Mac add decorations to the bright pink plastic tablecloth covering the long folding table that was to hold the party food. It had been a while since he'd seen his daughter so happy. As soon as she'd bounded out of bed this morning, she started cleaning and arranging, wanting everything to be just right. This party was important to her; therefore, it was important to him. But without Paisley, it wouldn't have happened at all. He owed her. Big-time. Even if he wasn't sure what that might look like.

On the ride home last night, his daughter had gone on and on about her time with Paisley, about how she'd taught Mac how to make the pretzels and swirl the icing on the cupcakes. Mac not only ate up the attention but enjoyed learning how to do things mothers and daughters typically did together, things he'd never be able to teach her.

He took a swig of his ice tea, still wondering what had Paisley so wound up last night. What made her want to escape and rush outside? She wasn't upset with Mac, so what was it? Had he done something?

No, he would have heard about it if he had. Whatever it was, she wasn't willing to open up. He just hoped she was in a better mood today.

Taking in the view from his hilltop perch, his gaze rolled beyond the pasture where horses grazed, and over the treetops. Before he knew it, he found himself frowning. Those dark clouds in the distance had better stay there. After all the planning and preparation Mac and Paisley had done for this party—not to mention how badly Mac had wanted this party in the first place— he'd hate to see it ruined.

He checked his watch, noting that it was almost four. The party started at five. Paisley should be here by now. She wouldn't stand Mac up, would she?

No, not after all they'd done yesterday. Of course, she'd sent most of the food home with them last night.

Mac's own mother repeatedly made promises she had no intention of keeping.

Except Paisley wasn't Shannon.

He couldn't ignore the growing relationship between Mac and Paisley, though. It was good for his daughter to have female role models in her life, right? And from what he could tell, Paisley was a strong, Godly woman, which would make her a good candidate. Still, what if she were to disappoint Mac?

When four fifteen rolled around and Paisley still wasn't there, his anxiety got the best of him. He pulled his phone from the pocket of his shorts and dialed her number, but it went straight to voice mail.

The doorbell rang as he was tucking the phone

into his pocket. *Lord, please let it be Paisley.* His long strides devoured the distance to the door. He jerked it open.

"Finally." He reached for the stack of foil pans in her arms. "What took you so long?"

Wearing white shorts and a blue tank top, she looked at him curiously before returning to the open hatch of her SUV. "I texted Mackenzie to let her know the mac and cheese balls were taking longer to fry than I expected." Holding a plastic container of cupcakes in one hand, she pressed a button to close the hatch with her other before returning to the house. "Didn't she tell you?"

"No." He closed the door behind her. "I wasn't aware you had her number."

Paisley continued into the kitchen, glancing over her shoulder. "We exchanged them yesterday. I wanted her to be able to contact me if she had any problems or questions." Depositing the cupcakes on the counter, she explained, "When I realized I was going to be late, I sent her instructions of what to do until I arrived."

Yet his knee-jerk reaction had been to think the worst. "Where should I put these?" He gestured to the pans.

"In the oven please. Two hundred degrees should be fine."

"You're here." A beaming Mac closed the patio door as she entered, then scurried toward Paisley.

"Of course, I am, darlin'." She embraced his daughter. "Now let's finish getting ready for this party before your guests arrive." They headed outside and set to work putting out decorations, party favors, plates and napkins. Paisley even added an inflatable palm tree to the pool.

"Whoa! That looks cool."

Crockett looked down from the window to find David standing beside him. "What brings you out of your dungeon? The smell of food?"

"I heard the doorbell and wanted to see if it was Ms. Paisley." His son was every bit as smitten with her as Mac was, and Paisley never failed to include him.

Mac and Paisley came back inside.

"David." Paisley gave him a hug. "Come with me. I need your help." In the kitchen, she opened the container that held the cupcakes. "Would you please sample one of these chocolate cupcakes and tell me if they're all right."

His blue eyes went wide. "Sure." He grabbed one.

"But we made strawberry," Mac said.

"We did. But there are a lot of chocolate lovers out there, so I made these this morning. Wouldn't want anyone to leave disappointed, right, David?" She sent the boy a wink as he took a big bite.

By five ten, all seven of Mac's guests had arrived and by five twenty they were all in the pool.

A smiling Paisley stood beside him. "They're having so much fun."

"Yes, they are. Thanks to you."

She peered up at him.

"Mac wouldn't have had a party at all if it wasn't for you."

Pink tinged her cheeks. "Trust me, the pleasure's all mine."

"Perhaps. But I just want you to know how much I appreciate everything you've done to make this happen."

Tilting her head, she watched him for a moment, making him wonder if she was questioning his sincerity. "You're welcome."

"I am a bit concerned, though."

"About what?"

He pointed beyond the pool. "Those clouds are getting closer. If I hear thunder, the girls are out of the pool. But what do we do then? They're here until eight o'clock, and there's only so much they can eat."

Paisley's gaze moved from him to the clouds and back. "Hmm. Let me think. Or maybe I'll just pray those clouds go the other way."

"And if they don't?"

"I said I'm thinking."

Crockett had just put the burgers on the grill when thunder rumbled, and lightning flickered across the sky. He let go a loud whistle to get the girls' attention. "Everyone out of the pool."

"But, Dad."

"No buts, Mac. There's lightning."

God punctuated his words with another flash.

"Aw, man," his daughter grumbled.

Crockett and Paisley hurried to move the food table into the house. Fortunately, there was no food on it yet.

By the time the rain began to pour, Mac and her friends were gathered around the kitchen table, eating and chatting as only young girls could.

Crockett leaned toward Paisley at the kitchen island. "What do we do when they're done eating?"

"Do you have any extra toilet paper?"

He couldn't help but laugh. "That was nowhere near what I was expecting you to say. You're joking, right?"

"Not at all. I have an idea, but I need to know what you have in the way of toilet paper." She bit into a mac and cheese ball.

"I don't know. I buy it at the warehouse place,

so it comes in a huge package. I probably have one unopened."

"Wonderful. I need at least eight rolls." She popped the remaining bite into her mouth.

Still uncertain, he lifted a brow. "For what?"

Her smile was a playful one. "You'll see. Unfortunately, you probably won't be able to reuse it, so I'll have to buy you some more."

"Don't worry about it. If this party is a success, it'll be worth it."

By the time the kids had finished their meals, Paisley had toilet paper rolls stacked in a pyramid on the coffee table.

"All right, ladies. Y'all come on in here."

"What's with the toilet paper?" Mac appeared more than a little skeptical.

"We're going to have a toilet paper fashion show."

Crockett's weren't the only set of eyebrows that went up.

"Each of you will be given a roll of toilet paper and you will have thirty minutes to create a runway-worthy outfit with it. So, you all put your heads together, get creative and let's see what you can come up with. Because there will be prizes."

The girls all looked at each other. "Cool!"

They each grabbed a roll of toilet paper.

"Oh," Paisley added, holding up a finger, "and

be prepared to strike your best model pose when you show off your creation."

The girls hurried down the hallway to Mac's room.

"David, do you want to play, too?" Paisley held up a roll of paper.

He adamantly shook his head. "Dad, can I watch TV in your room?"

"Go ahead, buddy."

David started to leave, then paused. "Ms. Paisley, could I have some more macaroni and cheese balls?"

"Of course you can. Just don't get any crumbs on your dad's bed."

As his son disappeared into the hallway behind the kitchen, Crockett watched Paisley clear plates and cups from the table. "You never miss a beat, do you?"

"What do you mean?"

"Nothing ruffles you. Instead, you move seamlessly from one thing to the next."

She dropped a stack of plates into the trash can. "Oh, I do plenty of ruffling. Didn't you see me last night?"

"Yes. Though I still don't know why." He hesitated for a split second, hoping she might elaborate. When she didn't, he went on. "But the running late, the rain, coming up with something fun for the girls to do—I still can't believe they went for the toilet paper thing, by the way. Even with David. Making him aware of the crumbs in a way that wasn't demeaning. You're patient, and your attention to detail is impeccable. Yet you make it look so simple."

"I've learned to be adaptable. And I'll take eight twelve-year-old girls over one bridezilla any day. Kids are much easier to please. Besides, they're with their friends, so they're going to have a ball no matter what they do. I need you to help me set up a catwalk, though. And we'll need some music."

"What kind of music?"

"Runway model music, of course."

"I don't even know what that is."

The corners of her mouth lifted. "I'll get my phone."

Thirty minutes later, the girls were strutting a path across his living room in their toilet paper garb. One girl looked like a mummy. And every last one of them was laughing and having the time of her life. If Paisley hadn't been here, they probably would have been in front of the television, staring blankly at the screen instead of interacting with each other. But thanks to her, they were genuinely having fun. The kind of fun that memories were made of.

Crockett watched Paisley as she presented the prizes—cellophane bags filled with a variety of candies and tied with ribbon—thinking how blessed Mackenzie and David were to have her in their lives.

What about you?

Paisley was a remarkable woman. Any guy would be blessed to have someone like her at their side. But she was out of his league. If he even had a league.

He gave himself a stern shake. What was he thinking? He didn't even want to play the game. Been there, done that, had the scars to prove it. Deep, ugly scars that made women like Paisley run away.

Mac and David might benefit from Paisley's attention. They were worth loving. But Crockett was another story. Notions of being anything other than Paisley's business partner were a waste of time, so he'd best accept it and move on down the road.

Chapter Eight

Paisley stared out the windows at the back of the castle Monday morning, her arms wound around her stomach, trying to hold herself together. The rain had started yesterday afternoon and continued ever since, intensifying overnight.

A weather alert on her phone had awakened her at three thirty this morning. When she'd looked at the screen and saw it was a river flood warning, she'd bolted out of bed, ready to head to the castle. It had flooded in the past, who's to say it wouldn't happen again. Everything on the first floor would have to be moved upstairs, just in case. Boxes, furniture…

She was already dressed and about to leave when Crockett called and all but ordered her to stay put. Though she'd tried to argue, his reminder that she wouldn't be able to see anything since there was no electricity had her acquiescing. So she killed time the only way she knew how. Baking.

Rae was surprised when she'd dropped off the oatmeal raisin and classic tollhouse cookies, along with some blond brownies, shortly after the café's six o'clock opening. It was there Paisley had run into Deputy Herne, who informed them flooding was already occurring upstream and it was only a matter of time before Bliss met the same fate. When he'd added that it was going to get even worse once they opened the floodgates in Austin, Paisley couldn't wait anymore.

Armed with a couple of flashlights and an LED lantern she kept for emergencies, she went to the castle. Though the sun had risen almost thirty minutes prior, between the rain and the darkened skies it was nearly impossible to see exactly where the water was. Since it had yet to reach the terrace, she'd texted Crockett to bring some sandbags, then began moving boxes of books upstairs to the ballroom.

Now, a little more than an hour later, with her muscles already protesting, she'd paused at the windows for another evaluation. In the four years she'd lived in Bliss, she'd never seen the river this high. Her insides twisted as the tempestuous waters inched up the lawn. And the rain showed no sign of letting up.

Checking the radar on her phone, she noted

that the entire region was one giant red blob. How much longer would they have?

With a frustrated breath, she returned to her work. Where was Crockett? He should be here by now. They needed to sandbag the doors and move furniture. Grabbing a side chair in each hand, she started up the stairs. *Lord, please don't allow the castle to be compromised. I can't bear to see another dream die.*

"Paisley?" Crockett's voice drifted from downstairs as she deposited the chairs in the ballroom.

"Coming." She descended the steps to find him at the back windows. "We've got a lot to do and not much time to do it. Did you get the sandbags?"

"That's what took me so long." He faced her as she came alongside him. "I had to stop by the hardware store. Fortunately, Christa was on top of things and her crew already had pallets of them filled and ready to go."

"Good, because as you can see—" she motioned to the scene outside "—we're going to need them."

He pulled off his rain jacket. "All right, then let's get to work."

They started with the furniture. The drop-leaf table in the library along with the two wingback chairs took both their efforts to move, as did the settee in the drawing room, the dining table and the sofa, upholstered chairs and coffee table in the family room. The knight's armor from the entry hall had been their greatest challenge. Not only was it heavy, it was precarious, to say the least.

By the time they'd finished with those items, Paisley was spent, yet there was still more to do. Looking at her watch, she was stunned to see that it was almost noon. She joined Crockett at a window. Water had leached onto the terrace.

"Can you get the rest of the furniture while I focus on the kitchen?"

"Yep. We'd better work fast." He went one way while she went the other.

No matter how exhausted she was, she couldn't afford to stop. Time was not on their side.

She'd emptied one cabinet when Crockett blew through the swinging door. "We have to get out of here."

Looking up from her position on the floor, she sent him a frustrated look. "Why?"

"They've opened the floodgates in Austin."

"Okay, but that won't reach us for at least twenty-four hours." She closed the cabinet door and stood. "I've barely touched the kitchen."

"Leave it."

"I can't do that. I have to at least try to save this stuff."

"There's nothing of value in here."

"How do you know?"

Annoyance pinched his brow as he stormed out the door.

Fine, let him be upset. She opened the next cupboard and grabbed another box. Just because Crockett was willing to give up so easily, didn't mean she had to. The Renwicks had entrusted the castle to her care, and she would treat it as though it belonged to her.

Midway through the third cabinet, her phone rang. She pulled it from her back pocket to see Molly's name on the screen. "Hello."

"Paisley, dear. Crockett apprised me of the situation in Bliss."

Her ire sparked. How dare he go tattling to Molly like a little boy. Sure, she needed to be kept abreast of the situation, she was the owner after all, but Paisley had planned to do that *after* everything had been relocated.

"I admire and appreciate your willingness to preserve Renwick Castle and its contents, however your life is much more valuable than the castle or anything in it. Do not put your life in danger trying to save worthless items."

Worthless? How could Molly say that? The castle was her legacy.

Crockett had obviously exaggerated the situation.

"No, of course not, Molly. I'm simply working to preserve everything I can."

"Crockett says they've released water from a dam upstream."

"That won't reach us for until tomorrow." Her battle right now was against the water currently encroaching.

"Are you certain?"

"Yes, ma'am."

There was a long pause. "All right. As long as you promise to exercise common sense."

Ending the call, Paisley went to find Crockett, eager to give him a piece of her mind. She moved into the entry hall and spotted him midway up the stairs with her last stack of empty boxes.

"I need those."

"No, you don't." He continued up the steps and disappeared around the corner. A moment later he reemerged. "You're done packing." He strode down the steps. "We need to leave."

She moved to the windows to again assess things. The water hadn't moved that much. She still had time.

Turning, she glared at Crockett. "You're overreacting. It's not like there's going to be some big wall of water sweeping through here like in the movies."

Hands perched on his hips, he glared back at her. "Have you ever been in a flood?"

"No."

"Then you have no idea how powerful moving water can be. Six inches will make it tough for you to walk to your vehicle without falling. A foot can float the vehicle. We have to get out of here while we still can."

Obviously, he didn't care about the castle as much as she did. He was blowing things out of proportion to try and scare her. Well, if he wanted to be a quitter, then so be it. But she was no quitter. She believed in fighting for what she wanted. Fighting for her dream. Something she never had the opportunity to do that dreadful Saturday five years ago when Peter and Logan were ripped away from her.

Tears filled her eyes. Unwilling to let Crockett see them, she turned back to the window. "Then you go. I have to stay and fight." Despite her blurred vision, she could see that the water now covered the terrace. How could it happen so fast?

"There is no fight, Paisley. Not against the forces of nature. We simply have to walk away and pray for the best."

"Walk away? Maybe you can do that, but I can't." A mixture of anger, exhaustion and frustration had her body trembling as tears spilled onto her cheeks. "What if something happens? What if I lose the castle like I lost Peter and Logan?" Her tears fell in earnest then, and she found herself cloaked in embarrassment. Had she actually said that out loud?

Though she refused to look at him, she knew the moment Crockett stepped in front of her. Seconds later, he enveloped her in his arms. Holding her close, he whispered soothing words and caressed her back.

She melted against him, allowing herself to savor his warmth and strength. And oh, how she missed it when he stepped back and looked her in the eye.

He brushed the hair away from her face. "Sweetheart, if Peter were here, I'm sure he would be telling you the same thing I am. He wouldn't allow you to put yourself in danger, and I'm not going to either. So you can walk out of here with me or I can carry you, but I cannot let you stay here any longer."

Paisley knew he was right. But she wasn't ready to admit defeat.

As if on cue, water began lapping at sandbags he'd placed outside the door. She'd done all she could and yet it wasn't enough. Unless God intervened, the castle would flood.

Her shoulders sagged as fresh tears blurred her vision. "I'll move that last box. Then we can go."

Wanting to make certain Paisley made it home safely, Crockett followed her back to her place.

Under normal circumstances, he would have driven her and come back later. But today he feared her vehicle might not be there when they came back.

Despite the windshield wipers slapping back and forth at a frenzied pace, he still found it difficult to see. Thankfully, Paisley's house wasn't that far away.

What if I lose the castle like I lost Peter and Logan?

Crockett had never been a hero kind of guy, wanting to swoop in and save the damsel in distress, but seeing Paisley's tears and hearing the pain in her voice had him wanting to not only protect her, but take away her pain. Paisley was a strong woman, perhaps one of the strongest women he'd ever met. She had to be to endure losing her spouse and her child. So to see her that defeated was unexpected, to say the least. And it had completely messed with his brain.

When they arrived at Paisley's, she drove into the garage while he parked behind her in the drive. He grabbed an umbrella and held it over her as she stepped into the rain. Despite the torrent, her steps were slow. He kept pace with her, glad they were both wearing rubber boots.

Her hands shook as she attempted to unlock the back door. He placed a steadying hand over hers and twisted the dead bolt.

Inside, she shrugged out of her raincoat. "I think I'll make some coffee." Rubbing her arms, she looked up at him. "Would you care for some? Or do you need to get home to the kids?"

He wasn't going anywhere until he knew she'd be okay. "The kids are fine with Ashley. And coffee would be great."

Paisley pulled coffee and a filter from the cupboard to the left of the sink, her hands still shaky. When she almost dropped the glass carafe, he stepped in.

"Why don't you sit down. I can take care of this."

Her smile was weak, and he was surprised when she said, "Thank you."

Instead of heading for the table or the living room, she disappeared into the laundry room and returned moments later, wrapped in a bulky sweater. She continued toward the table, releasing the clip from her hair, sending her coppery waves spilling around her shoulders.

He found himself wondering if they were as soft as they looked. Then chided himself for thinking something so crazy.

Retrieving two mugs from the same cupboard the coffee was in, he said, "Cream or sugar?"

"There's creamer in the refrigerator."

After locating it, he joined her at the table. She added a small amount of the vanilla-flavored cream, wrapped her long fingers around the Georgia Bulldogs mug and watched the dark liquid turn a pale brown. "We were getting ready to leave for vacation. Logan had been begging Peter and me to take him to Disney World ever since he was old enough to know what it was."

Crockett wasn't sure where that had come from or why Paisley had decided to share it with him. Normally he'd shy away from something so personal, not to mention emotional. Yet he found himself wanting her to share. Wanting her to know that he was there for her.

"I'd stayed up late the night before, doing laundry and packing," she continued. "When I woke up the next morning, Peter had left a note on my bathroom mirror, letting me know that he and Logan had gone to Krispy Kreme and they'd be back soon."

She sipped her coffee. "I showered and got ready for the day, and when they still weren't back I called Peter, but he didn't answer. The trip shouldn't have taken them more than twenty to thirty minutes, depending on the line, and it had been almost an hour since I'd found the note. So I kept calling, but it kept going to voice mail." Her gaze shifted to the window, and she simply stared. "Finally, I got into my car and drove the route I knew they would have taken. A block before the doughnut shop, I saw flashing lights.

And as I slowed down, I saw a tangled heap of metal wrapped around a light pole in the median. I slammed my car into Park, not caring that I was in the middle of the road, and hurried toward the wreckage. An officer stopped me. I told him that was my husband's car and that he and my son had gone to get doughnuts."

Her shoulders lifted briefly as she drew in a shaky breath. "I will never forget the look on the officer's face as it morphed from intense to sympathetic. And then his voice cracked when he said, 'I'm sorry, ma'am.'"

Longing to give her some sort of comfort, Crockett reached across the table and took hold of her hand.

She latched on to it as though it were a lifeline. "A distracted driver had run a red light and plowed into Peter's car going forty-five miles per hour in a thirty-five zone. The police said they didn't stand a chance." A lone tear spilled ono her cheek, tearing at Crockett's heart. "I never even got to say goodbye."

Crockett cleared his throat and somehow managed to talk around the lump that was still lodged there. "I am so sorry you had to go through that, Paisley."

"Me, too." She lifted a shoulder and made a poor attempt at a smile. "And just so you know, I don't usually tell people that story." She finally made eye contact with him. "But since I kind of exposed my heart back there at the castle, I thought you deserved to know."

Still holding her hand, he roughed a thumb over her knuckles. "How did you end up in Bliss?"

"I shut down Weddings by Paisley soon after the accident. I wasn't in any shape to plan weddings or give pep talks to brides-to-be, let alone run a business. Once I stopped wallowing in my grief, I knew I had to begin anew. That my dreams no longer centered around my family. That it was time to think about me and what I wanted. But my family and friends made that rather difficult."

"How so?"

"This probably sounds terrible, but I grew weary of their pity."

"Not at all. I've been there myself."

"I know they meant well, but as soon as I'd take two steps forward, they'd pull me back. So, I decided to relocate. I didn't know where, didn't particularly care, so long as it was where God wanted me to be." She smiled in earnest then. "I was at the doctor's office one day, thumbing through a magazine, when I saw a sweet little ad for this charming town in Texas. Knowing that I definitely needed a little bliss in my life, as the ad said, I visited and fell in love with the town and its people."

"Do you ever miss the city?"

She puffed out a laugh. "There are many things I miss, but the city is not one of them."

He studied the remarkable woman across from him. "Paisley, I believe I owe you an apology."

"For what?"

Still holding her hand, he stood, rounded the table and pulled her to her feet. "For underestimating you. You are a strong woman, stronger than most men. Myself included."

"I highly doubt that."

"I don't. The fact that you were able to move past your pain and start a new life here in Bliss, all the while holding tight to your faith, is something to be admired. It makes me ashamed of how I treated you in the past."

"Now who's pitying me?"

"Paisley, the only pitiful one here is me." It really bugged him, the way his hackles used to go up whenever he was around her.

"That's not true. You're a good man." She released his hand and moved toward the window. "This rain isn't going to let up anytime soon. What do we do about the castle?"

"We wait. It may be a few days before we can get back in there."

Yawning, she nodded. "I think I need a nap."

At least her mood seemed to have improved, so he wouldn't have to worry about leaving her while she was down. Problem was, he didn't want to go. Like someone who'd just uncovered a rare treasure, he wanted to stay and admire it.

And that was a problem he'd never anticipated.

Chapter Nine

Bile burned the back of Paisley's throat as she stood in the open doorway of the castle late Wednesday morning. When Crockett suggested the water had receded enough for them to safely check on things at the castle, she'd been more than eager. But she definitely wasn't prepared. Mud and muck stretched the length of the entry hall and beyond.

"I think I might be sick." She pressed a hand to her stomach.

Crockett stepped inside. "I'd say we got off pretty easy." Crouching, he eyed the area where the floor met the wall. "Doesn't look like we had more than six inches." He stood. "Could have been much worse."

"I don't even want to think about what that would have looked like." Wearing her rubber boots, she moved into the entry hall before making a left into the library. Things hadn't fared any better in there. "Good thing we took those drapes down."

They wandered from room to room, assessing the damage, which was pretty much the same no matter where they went on the first level. Mud-covered floors, small puddles, dank air. Far more than a mop or a fan could cure.

"I'm glad there wasn't any carpeting down here." She continued into the kitchen where her packing had come to a halt. "This looks even more disgusting than it did before."

"Good news." Crockett moved behind her. "It was slated to be a gut job anyway."

"What do we do about all this mud? Shovel? Shop-Vac?"

"No, we're leaving this to the professionals. Molly's already given me the go-ahead to bring in remediation specialists—" He grabbed her elbow and tugged her toward him. "Looks like we have a guest."

"A guest?" She peered up at him. "What do you mean a—?"

His gaze was intent.

Following his stare, she saw something slithering near one of the cupboards. A shudder ran through her as she took another step back. "Is it poisonous?"

"Yep. It's a cottonmouth." His dark eyes still

fixed on the snake, he said, "Hand me that broom by the door."

Reaching behind her, she grabbed the old wooden broom and handed it to him. "How are you going to kill it with that?"

Armed, he took a step forward. "Why don't you open that door." He nodded toward the corner of the kitchen. "Then come on back here behind me."

"Why? What are you—?"

"Door please." His voice was calm as he nudged the snake with the end of the handle—something the snake did not take kindly to.

"How do I know that isn't where he came from or that there aren't any more?"

"Paisley. Please."

She huffed out a breath, grabbed the phone from her pocket and turned on the flashlight before cautiously approaching the area. Satisfied it was clear, she pulled the door open and hurried back toward the swinging door.

"Thaaank you." He slowly lifted the broom handle, bringing the snake with it. Then he inched toward the door, holding the broom steady, his focus never leaving the nasty creature.

When he stepped outside, she moved closer to see him lower the snake into the grass. Then he hurried back inside, closing the door behind him.

Hand on her hip, Paisley looked up at him. "I

can't believe you let him go. That was a poisonous snake. Why didn't you kill it?"

He stared down at her, his expression stern. "Would you have preferred I let you handle it?"

"Of course not. Though I probably would have bludgeoned it with the broom. Or at least tried."

"Uh-huh. Well, I didn't have a shotgun or shovel, so I had to improvise, all right?"

She couldn't help smiling. "My hero."

"Whatever." He pushed past her. "Let's go grab some lunch at Rae's. I'm getting cranky."

"What else is new," she mumbled, following him through the swinging door. "But we need to come up with a plan of action."

"I think better on a full stomach."

After locking up, she climbed into his truck, and they rode in silence.

Five minutes later, he pushed open the door of the café, allowing Paisley to enter.

The aroma of coffee mingled with the tantalizing scents of fried chicken and beef enchiladas, making her stomach growl. Since it wasn't quite noon, they had their pick of tables.

Behind the counter, Rae was conversing with one of her waitresses. And it appeared the waitress was crying.

Just then, Rae looked their way. "Paisley, come on over here."

Peering up at Crockett, she lifted a shoulder. "Let's see what's up."

Rae addressed the young woman beside her. "If anyone can help us figure this out, it's Paisley."

"What do we need to figure out?" She glanced from Rae to the waitress.

"Samantha is supposed to get married on Saturday."

"I heard." Paisley couldn't help smiling. "Congratulations."

"Well, there's been a little mishap." Rae eyed a weeping Samantha. "The roof on the parish hall collapsed from all of the rain. They were supposed to have their reception there."

"Oh, no. That's terrible." Paisley's heart went out to the girl. "I'm so sorry, sweetie."

The young woman sniffed. "If we can't find someplace else, we'll have to cancel the wedding."

"Nonsense." Paisley reached across the counter and squeezed her hand. "I'm sure one of the other churches in town would be happy to step in."

"None of them are big enough. Besides, all of our decorations were in the hall. Now they're ruined."

Releasing Samantha, Paisley mentally sifted through other prospective venues, trying to come up with a solution. "Now don't you go giving up hope just yet. Decorations can be replaced, and there's bound to be some place in this area that will work. What about Cattleman's Hall?"

Samantha looked chagrinned. "We can't afford it."

"I understand. Even if you could, it's rather plain. The parish hall has a nice ambiance."

"That's why we were going to have it there. Well, that and the church gave us a discount. But I wanted a rustic wedding."

"Rustic, huh?" An image popped into Paisley's head. "Excuse me for a minute." She tugged a rather uncomfortable-looking Crockett aside. "Didn't I see an old wooden barn out at your place?"

"Yeah. We use it to store hay."

"So, it's structurally sound?"

"Of course." His brow wrinkled.

"Does it have electricity?"

His gaze narrowed. "I'm almost afraid to say yes."

"Great, can I see it?"

"When?"

"Right now."

"Paisley, if you're thinking what I think you're thinking—"

She grabbed him by the arm. "Come on. We can talk while you drive."

"Now, just hold on a second." He tugged free. "I'm hungry."

"Oh, all right." She looked over her shoulder. "Rae, I need two burgers and fries to go. And the faster the better."

"I'm on it."

Rejoining Samantha, she said, "Don't give up hope just yet, darlin'. Not until you hear back from me."

"You know, I had my heart set on the fried chicken special." With one hand on the steering wheel and a burger in the other, Crockett whizzed past the Bliss city limit sign.

"And I wanted you to kill that snake, so we'll call it even." In the passenger seat, Paisley popped a shoestring fry in her mouth.

"You sure seemed eager to help that girl with her plight. Like something sparked to life inside of you."

"Yeah, it did." A sweet smile played across her lips as she peered out the window at the waterlogged pastureland. "When I closed the doors on Weddings by Paisley, I didn't think I'd ever want to go back. That it would be too painful. But this past year I found myself missing it." She looked back at him. "Then on a walk one day, I wandered by the castle. I started doing a little research and, well, here we are."

"Until you mentioned Weddings by Paisley the other day, I wasn't aware that you'd owned a wedding planning business."

"I've been smitten with weddings all my life, and God gave me the skills to help make bridal dreams come true. Weddings by Paisley drew clients from all over Georgia."

He glanced her way. "Impressive."

"To some people, maybe. I just loved what I did."

"And you're seriously considering having a wedding reception in my barn?"

"I won't know if it's doable until I see it. If it is, would you allow Samantha and Brenden to use it? I promise to oversee everything and will take full responsibility if anything is damaged." She peeled back the wrapper on her burger. "I just hate the thought of them having to postpone their wedding because they don't have a place for their reception."

His own burger gone, he retrieved his foam cup of water from the cupholder. "Why don't they just have the wedding and call it good?"

"Because the wedding is formal, whereas the reception is relaxed. It allows the happy couple to mingle with their guests and celebrate with friends and family."

"Wow. My wedding reception wasn't anything like that."

She twisted to face him. "What do you mean?"

"Ninety-five percent of the two hundred guests were Shannon's friends and family. And since I wasn't much of a dancer, she spent most of the night on the dance floor with her friends."

"Crockett, that's horrible." Reaching across the center console, she squeezed his arm, sending a jolt of awareness straight to his heart. "A wedding and the reception are supposed to be about the couple, not just one person. That's something I always emphasized to my brides. Even though they get to be a princess for the day, the wedding isn't just about them. The man they intend to spend the rest of their life with needs to be happy, too."

Crockett couldn't help the laugh that puffed out. "Maybe that was part of Shannon's problem."

"What?"

"I don't think she planned to spend the rest of her life with me. Once the party was over and life became day-to-day, she lost interest. Said I was boring."

"Surely there were some good times."

"I suppose. Things were pretty good when she was pregnant with Mac. I think it was mostly because it made Shannon the center of attention. But again, the newness wore off a few months after Mac was born."

"What about David?"

His heart squeezed. He pulled in a long breath while the hum of the tires filled the air. "Shannon was not happy when she learned she was pregnant a second time. After David was born, she insisted we hire a nanny because she couldn't be expected to stay at home with two kids all day. I told her she'd have to go back to work then, but that didn't last."

"So what did she do?"

"Before or after she found a boyfriend?"

"Oh, Crockett." He'd never seen such a cute pout. "That's terrible. How did you end up with someone like that?"

He lifted a shoulder. "She was very convincing. Fortunately, I had a better lawyer than she did, so she didn't walk away with near as much money as she thought she would."

"Well, I find that very infuriating. I mean, it's one thing to 'fall out of love'—" she did air quotes "—with someone, but to go after their money is just plain spiteful."

"Ah, it's all right. She found herself a sugar daddy who seems more than happy to cater to her every whim."

Paisley shook her head. "It hurts my heart that you had to go through that. Those must have been some tough years." As if she hadn't had her share of those.

"They were, but I try not to dwell on them. Not when I have Mac and David. They're the best things that ever happened to me."

"They're great kids. You've done a good job with them. I'm just sorry you have to go it alone."

"I don't know. Parenting may not be easy but, in my experience, it's a lot easier than marriage ever was. I'm not planning to go down that road again."

"You shouldn't close yourself off to love just because of one bad experience."

"Once bitten, twice shy." No woman in her right mind would want him, anyway. He hadn't even been good enough for his own mother, and now that he'd revealed so much to Paisley, she'd see him for the loser he was. If she hadn't figured it out already.

He pulled into the ranch, allowing the country music from the radio to fill the space as they continued past the house, following the road beyond the horse barns and along the edge of the pasture before coming to a stop in front of the gable-roofed structure with faded red paint.

Paisley stepped out of the truck, her sapphire eyes alight with wonder. "This is even better up close." Her attention shifted to him. "If the inside is half as good as the outside, we might have a winner." Her excitement was contagious.

He eagerly slid the doors open, an unexpected

thrill welling inside of him as though she'd been talking about him instead of the barn. Like that would ever happen.

Inside, she took in the dark gray rafters, beams and posts. "Now, this is how rustic is supposed to look. All we'd really need to do is get the hay out of here, clean things up, string some lights. Lots of lights." Pausing in the center of the space, she turned right, then left. "We could have a dance floor here in the middle." She motioned with her hands. "Tables and chairs all around it. Table-cloths. Mason jars full of wildflowers. That is, assuming they didn't drown." Smiling, she nodded. "Mmm-hmm. This should be quite spacious without the hay." She pulled out her phone, made a few taps, then let out an emphatic, "Yes!"

"What are we yessing about?"

"I was checking the weather. Things look good for Saturday night, so we could put some tables outside, too. Overflow for those wanting to escape the noise inside."

"Yeah, I can see that. I, uh, might even be able to come up with a few wooden picnic tables. You know, to keep that rustic feel going."

"I love it!" She approached him. "Crockett, I know I kind of forced this on you, but what do you say? Can Samantha and Brenden have their wedding reception here?"

"Are you sure? I mean, it has a dirt floor."

"At least it's dry."

"What about air-conditioning? It doesn't have that."

"Do you have any of those industrial fans in the horse barns?"

He couldn't help smiling. The animated way she described things had him wanting to see her vision come to life. "A couple of them."

"So... What do you think?"

He stepped closer, taking in that sweet fragrance that was uniquely Paisley. "I think there are only three days until their wedding, so we'd best get to work."

Chapter Ten

"This is so exciting!" Standing beside a long folding table inside of the old barn Saturday morning, Mackenzie placed another wildflower bouquet into a mason jar. "I can't believe there's going to be a wedding here."

Paisley was rather surprised, too. After hearing about Crockett's wedding, she'd feared he might refuse. What sort of bride chooses her friends over her groom?

One who can walk away from her children without a second glance.

She shook her head. There were some things in this world she'd never understand.

Learning about Crockett's past made her even more appreciative when he agreed to allow Samantha and Brenden to have their reception here. The thought of watching all those months of planning suddenly slip away broke her heart. She was determined to do everything in her power to make certain this reception was every bit as special as the one they'd planned and provide them the perfect opportunity to share their special day with family and friends.

"I so appreciate your help, Mackenzie." Assembling another grouping of daisies, prairie verbena, rain lilies and sunflowers they'd gathered around the ranch last night, Paisley couldn't help thinking what a huge help Crockett and his children had been these past couple of days. From the moment Samantha agreed to their offer, it was game on. They needed seating, decorations and countless other items. Phone calls were made. The bride and groom contacted family and friends.

When Paisley arrived at the ranch Thursday morning, armed with every string of lights she could get her hands on, Crockett had already removed the hay bales. Then they'd raked up the remaining scraps from the dirt floor before wrapping every brace, beam and post with tiny white lights. Next, they'd crisscrossed strings of patio lights to form a canopy over the entire space.

Friday, Paisley, Crockett and the kids had picked up tables, chairs and table coverings from the church where the reception was originally scheduled to take place, as well as a wooden dance floor from some friends of the bride's parents. The rest of the afternoon was spent unloading and arranging everything in the barn. Then, after a quick supper, they'd roamed the ranch in search of wildflowers.

"It doesn't feel like work when it's fun." Mackenzie watched Paisley add another lily to her mix. "And I always have fun when I'm with you." Her words warmed Paisley's heart.

"Aw, I feel the same way about you, sweet thing." She twisted a piece of jute around the flower bundle. "Which reminds me, depending on how things are going at the castle, perhaps we could make that trip to the city in a couple of weeks."

The girl's dark eyes sparkled as an engine ground to a halt outside the door. "That would be awesome!"

They both looked up as Crockett and David strolled through the door, each carrying a stack of wood slices Crockett had cut from a downed post oak to be used as pedestals for the flower arrangements on each of the tables.

"How're things goin' in here?" Crockett set his stack on a nearby table then motioned for his son to do the same.

"I'm running out of flowers." Wiping her brow, Paisley eyed her dwindling pile of blooms. She thought she'd had an adequate supply, but each quart-size jar required more than she'd anticipated. "There are six jars left and only enough flowers for one and a half."

"David and I can get you some more. Just as soon as we finish unloading the wood pieces."

"Would you? That would save me so much time."

"Just tell me what you need."

"Mostly daisies and verbena. Though you can always bring more lilies. After all that rain, there are tons of those."

"Got it. Come on, David. We've got work to do."

Once the wood was unloaded, Crockett grabbed one of the five-gallon buckets they'd used for the flowers and moments later the Ranger sprang to life and sped away as her phone vibrated in her back pocket.

With one hand full of flowers, she tugged it from her shorts with the other. "Hello?"

"Is this Paisley?"

"Yes."

"Deidra Smith here. I'm doing the cakes for Samantha and Brenden's wedding."

"Yes, ma'am." Samantha had told her to expect a call.

"I'm just lettin' y'all know that I'll be headed your way right after lunch."

"Oh, I wasn't expecting you so early." They had yet to dress the tables. And she'd hate to mess up the cakes while they were working.

"Will you be there?"

With all the work still left to do? "Yes, we will definitely be here." She gave the woman directions.

"All right, sugar, I'll see you soon."

Ending the call, Paisley tucked the phone away and set the flowers down. "Mackenzie, it looks like we're going to cover the tables while we wait for the flowers." She opened the large black trash bag the woman at the church had given them, reached in and pulled out a small stack of tablecloths. She took one for the cake table, then passed the rest to the girl. "Here you go, darlin'. Start wherever you like."

Moving to the table positioned prominently near the back wall, Paisley unfurled the cloth and settled it over the hard-plastic surface.

"Something's wrong with this one."

Turning, she saw Mackenzie approach, holding a white tablecloth peppered with black spots. "Well, that won't do. Set it aside and get another one out of the bag." She smoothed out the creases as the girl walked away.

"Eww!"

"What is it?" Paisley rushed toward the girl.

Nose wrinkled, Mackenzie held up another discolored cloth. "It smells gross."

Paisley's gut tightened. Upending the bag onto one of the tables, her suspicions were confirmed.

"They're all damp and moldy." She stared at the speckled heap. "They must've been stored somewhere near the roof collapse. Obviously, no one checked to make sure they were all right."

"Can you wash them?"

"We haven't got time." She returned to the cake table, eyeing the blessedly spotless covering. Grabbing hold of a corner, she brought it to her nose and sniffed. "At least this one's okay." Though she had no idea where she was going to find twenty tablecloths at the last minute.

Her phone vibrated again.

With a sigh, she looked at the screen. "Hey, Rae."

"Calling to let you know that I'll be on my way as soon as the lunch crowd clears. And everything will be in coolers to keep it warm or cold, so they can stay there until it's time to eat." While the groom's grandfather was providing the smoked brisket and sausage, Rae handled the side dishes for the reception.

"Sounds great." Her gaze fell to the smelly pile on the table. "I don't suppose you have any rectangular tablecloths, do you?"

"Yeah, I use them when I cater."

Hope sifted through Paisley. "How many?"

"Three dozen. I got them on clearance from one of the supply houses."

"Could I borrow them? The ones the church gave us are all moldy."

"Certainly. But I should warn you that they're black."

"Oh, bless you. And don't worry, I'll make them work."

After giving her friend directions, she ended the call with a sigh of relief and looked across the way to Mackenzie. "Rae's bringing tablecloths, so let's put these foul things back in the bag."

By the time they'd finished, Crockett and David had returned.

"I think you're going to be happy." Crockett set the overflowing bucket on the table. "We found more verbena, so I brought extra."

"Oh, you have no idea how happy that makes me." Without thinking, she pushed up on her toes and kissed his cheek, his stubble tickling her lips. "Thank you so much."

It wasn't until she saw the stunned look on his face that she realized what she'd done.

She quickly turned away, her cheeks heating. "Another crisis averted." A goofy laugh accompanied her words. Why on earth had she kissed Crockett? In front of his children, no less. That wasn't like her. When had she become so comfortable with him that she'd do something so bold?

"There've been more?" he asked.

Focused on the nosegays, she explained about the tablecloths, trying to behave as though everything was normal. As if kissing Crockett or any other man was normal.

"Good." He seemed to have recovered. "I'm glad Rae could help." He looked from her to his daughter. "If y'all are good here, David and I are gonna run up to the house and fix us all some sandwiches." No doubt, he was probably eager to escape.

Paisley trimmed a verbena stem. "Sounds good to me." Lord willing, the butterflies swarming her stomach would settle before he returned.

"Don't forget chips," Mackenzie added. A short time later, after the guys drove away, she said, "Do you like my dad?"

Paisley managed to keep her groan to herself. "We're friends, yes, and business partners."

"But you kissed him."

"I did. But not for reasons you might think." She added jute to another bouquet. "Have you ever done something unusual because you were excited?"

"Like when I almost knocked you over when Dad said you'd help with my party?"

The knotted mass in Paisley's stomach relaxed. "Yes. After the problem with the tablecloths, I was so relieved to see that we not only had flowers, but extra flowers, that I got a little overzealous." She handed the finished bouquet to Mackenzie.

"Well—" the girl eased it into a mason jar "—I wouldn't have cared if it was a real kiss. I think it would be cool if you and my dad, you know—" she lifted a shoulder "—started dating."

Regret over her actions quadrupled in that moment. How could she have acted so carelessly? It was only natural Crockett's children would assume she liked their father in a romantic way. Women don't just go around kissing men they're not attracted to. But then, that could only mean one thing.

She was attracted to Crockett. And that couldn't happen.

Darkness had descended on the ranch, and night sounds filled the warm evening air as Crockett and Paisley stood just outside of the open door of the barn.

"We can't thank you all enough." While the DJ played another country tune, a wedding dress–clad Samantha held her groom's hand. "This was ten times better than the parish hall."

Wearing dark washed Levi's topped with a light brown vest over a white button-down, Brenden looked from the rafters to the dance floor and all around. "I still can't believe you did all of this in only three days."

"You have this lady to thank for that." Crockett nodded toward Paisley, who stood beside him, looking far too beautiful in a blue-and-white sundress that made her eyes sparkle. "She had the vision. The kids and I were simply the minions who helped her execute it."

She bumped him with her elbow. "Don't be so modest. This is your barn after all."

"Dude—" Brenden shot him a look "—you saved the day by allowing us to have our reception here." Slipping a hand around his bride's waist, he tugged her close and stared into her eyes. "Thanks to you, we didn't have to postpone our wedding."

"And for that, I will be forever grateful." Samantha faced them, her smile wide. "You two are amazing."

"She is." Crockett poked a thumb in Paisley's direction. "I just did whatever she told me to."

"It's about time for us to head out," said Brenden. "But I think the two of you should take a break and enjoy the party."

"That's right." His wife nodded. "Eat. Dance. Enjoy the fruits of your labor."

Dancing with Paisley? Now, there was a thought sure to have Crockett battling with himself. After the peck she'd given him this morning, he didn't know how to react. So he hadn't. At least not on the outside. Inside, though, he was jumping for joy all the while shaking in his boots. Her innocent kiss had unleashed emotions he'd never expected nor wanted to feel again. Hopes and dreams wrestled with heartaches and disappointments. Things he'd longed for, things that would never be.

Still, after all she'd done to make this an event Brenden and Samantha would always remember, Crockett wanted Paisley to enjoy herself. So once the bride and groom departed, he said, "You know, the happy couple might be on to something. I haven't seen you on the dance floor all night." He'd at least danced with Mac.

Pink colored her cheeks as she scooped up a plastic plate someone had left on the edge of the gift table. "That's because I've been working."

"Well, you know what they say about that."

She peered up at him.

"All work and no play makes Paisley a dull girl." As if she could ever be dull.

The slow notes of a guitar and fiddle began to play, so Crockett held out his hand. "Care to join me?"

For a split second, she looked nervous. Then one brow lifted in question. "I thought you didn't dance."

"I said I'm not much of a dancer. I don't do freestyle. However, I can slow dance with the best of 'em."

After a long moment—long enough to have him second-guessing his decision—she smiled and placed her hand in his.

When they stepped onto the dance floor, he slipped one arm around her waist and pulled her close, holding her other hand against his chest. Mercy, she smelled good. Like sugar and spice and everything nice. Except Paisley wasn't a little girl. She was a vivacious woman. Strong and independent. Not to mention gorgeous. Things he would typically discount. But the heart behind those things was like a siren, beckoning him to forget his vow to steer clear of women.

While lights twinkled overhead, he shook away the thought. "You know, Mac is already talking about having a dance party in here."

The corners of her suddenly enticing mouth lifted. "She and her friends would have a ball."

"David wants one, too. Without the dancing, though."

"Of course he does." Her hand moved gently over his shoulder.

"You know what this means, don't you?"

She gave the slightest shake of her head.

"It means I may never get my hay barn back."

Her laughter washed over him, breathing life into his dormant heart.

"And it's all your fault."

"My fault?" Her body stiffened beneath his fingers.

"If you hadn't made my barn look so appealing, no one would be wanting parties in here."

Her shoulders relaxed, her gaze drifting to his. "You could have said no, you know."

"And face the wrath of the wedding planner?" He shook his head. "No way. Because I'd much rather see her smile." His words had her doing just that.

"I'm glad we were able to do this. Not only for Samantha and Brenden, but because it took my mind off the castle and gave me something else to focus on."

"And you'll have a day to rest before heading back into the castle." They'd spoken with Wes Bishop, a local contractor and the husband of one of Paisley's friends, who'd agreed to meet with them Monday.

"A day to recover will be nice." Her yawn seemed to emphasize her point.

"Why don't you go on home? We can clean up tomorrow."

"No, I'm all right."

"I'm not buying that. You've been here since dawn."

"I wanted everything to be perfect."

"And it was." Much like her. "I have to admit, I was skeptical."

"You skeptical? No way."

"All right, sassy." Releasing her hand, he swept a lock of that gorgeous red hair away from her face. "What you did here… You have a gift, Paisley. Not everyone can take a run-down barn and turn it into something beautiful."

"Oh, this barn is not run-down."

"Still, you heard what Samantha said. This was better than what they'd originally planned."

She was quiet for a moment. "That's why I enjoy planning weddings. Seeing the awestruck looks on the couples' faces and knowing that I made their dreams come true is very satisfying."

If he were a better man, he'd do everything in his power to make her dreams come true. "You're an amazing woman, Paisley. I'm sorry I ever doubted you."

She smiled up at him. "Consider it a lesson learned."

For a moment, everything and everyone faded away as Crockett lost himself in her sapphire eyes. His gaze drifted to her lips, curiosity niggling its way into his traitorous brain. If he lowered his head just a little more—

"Dad?" Mac touched his elbow.

Paisley promptly took a step back.

He rubbed the back of his neck. "What is it, Mac?" And why couldn't it have waited until the dance was over?

"David's asleep."

There was no place to lie down in here. "Where?"

His daughter pointed to one of the tables.

"Aw, sweet baby," said Paisley.

His son was sitting in a chair, arms folded atop the table, his head cradled on top of them. "Little guy is tuckered out."

"Why don't you go ahead and take him back to the house?" Paisley looked from David to Crockett. "Now that the bride and groom are gone their guests will start to dwindle."

"I can't leave you to do the cleanup alone."

"Both families have already said they would help, so I'll be fine."

He didn't want to leave her. On the contrary, he still wanted her in his arms on the dance floor. But then, who knew what would happen. He'd almost kissed her. He'd wanted to. Still wanted to. And that wasn't like him.

But then, Paisley was unlike any woman he'd ever met. Leaving his heart and his brain in a big ol' tug-of-war. And at this moment, he wasn't sure which one would win.

Chapter Eleven

Paisley's phone vibrated next to her on the bed Sunday afternoon, rousing her from a much-needed nap, one beset with dreams of being held in Crockett's arms and giving in to his kiss. Meaning whoever was on the other end of the phone line had her utmost gratitude.

Rolling over, she lifted the phone to see her parents' image on the screen. Unease rose inside of her, but she answered anyway. "Hello." She flopped back on the pillow.

"Hi, sweet pea!"

"Hi, Mama."

"How are you, peanut?"

"I'm doing well, Daddy."

"You don't sound like you're doing well. Ralph, she doesn't sound well, does she?" Leave it to Barbara June Cummings to read something into nothing. "Are you sad, sweet pea? You haven't been cryin', have you?" It had been five years since Peter and Logan went home to be with Jesus, yet her mother still thought Paisley was in mourning 24/7.

"No, Mama. I was taking a nap." Swinging her legs over the side of the queen-size bed, she sat up, brushing her hair away from her face.

"Why?"

"Because I was tired. I oversaw a wedding last night and got in late."

"Did you go to church?"

"Yes, Mama. I teach Sunday school, remember?" She fought the urge to pull one of Mackenzie's eye rolls. "Then I came straight home, ate a bite and lay down."

"Oh." Why did her mother have to sound so disappointed? As if it was wrong for Paisley to have a life.

"Barbara June, stop interrogating the poor girl." Paisley couldn't help but smile. Her father had always been eager to come to her defense. No wonder he was her original knight in shining armor. "Paisley, I promise you that is not why we called."

As if every other phone call didn't start out in a similar manner. "What's going on with y'all?"

"We're fixin' to go RVing again," said her mother. "And we thought we'd make a swing through Texas so we could stop by and see Y-O-U."

Try as she might, Paisley couldn't muster any enthusiasm for the announcement. Ever since Peter and Logan's deaths, her parents, particularly her mother, had perpetually pitied her, as though Paisley was helpless to live without them. Mama's constant doting and placating were why Paisley moved to Texas. Yes, she'd gone through the grieving process like any wife and mother would, but it wasn't her heartache that kept her from moving forward in Georgia. It was her parents.

"I know how y'all love to travel." Standing, she slid the louvers on the plantation shutters open, the bright sun making her squint.

"Well, peanut, this country of ours is far too big to cover in one trip."

Perhaps they wouldn't stay long, then. "When should I expect you?"

"Wednesday afternoon," said Mama. "Now, I don't want you to go making a big fuss. We can sleep in the RV and do our own cookin'."

With a shake of her head, Paisley said, "Mama, you know you raised me better than that. I may not kill the fattened calf, but I do live in a bed-and-breakfast so there's no need to sleep elsewhere."

"Are you sure, sweet pea?"

She tucked her phone between her shoulder and ear, grabbed the throw from the bed and folded it. "If I came to visit you in an RV, where would you expect me to sleep, Mama?"

"In your old room, of course."

"So why should you visiting me be any different?" She set the throw aside.

"Now, there's no need to get testy, young lady."

If they thought she was testy now, just wait until she'd had twenty-four hours with them. "I can't wait to show y'all the castle."

"I reckon that's been keepin' you busy, huh?" Again with the disappointment. Why couldn't her mother just be happy for her?

"Things are finally gettin' rolling." She wasn't about to mention the flood. That could wait.

A beep alerted her to another call. Looking at the screen, she saw Crockett's name. Without the slightest hesitation she said, "My business partner is calling so I need to let y'all go. I'll see you Wednesday."

"All right, bye, sweet pea."

"Bye, peanut."

"Drive safe."

Since when do you dream about kissing a business partner? her conscience prodded as she switched calls.

"Hello."

"I didn't wake you, did I?"

She quickly tamped down the unwanted thrill his concern elicited. "No, my parents had that honor. Looks like they're going to be paying me a visit. They said they'd be here Wednesday."

"I get the feeling you're not too happy about that."

"I'll be all right. They just frustrate me sometimes." Wandering out of her room and toward the kitchen where there was a slice of wedding cake with her name on it, she did her best to keep things light. "So what's up?"

"I promised the kids La Familia for dinner, and they begged me to invite you to join us."

In that moment, her hesitation wasn't only because of Crockett. All the time she'd spent with him and his children this past week reminded her how much she missed having a family. Add to that Mackenzie's desire to know if Paisley liked her dad, and she suddenly found herself wondering if she shouldn't back off a bit and limit her time with them.

Then again, if she did that, Mackenzie would have no adult female influence in her life. No one she felt comfortable talking to about girl things. She'd be a teenager soon, and it was better for her to get advice from an adult she trusted rather than her peers. Still…

"Crockett, I—"

"Please don't say no. Otherwise I'll never hear the end of it, and I won't be able to enjoy my dinner."

She chuckled, her reasoning evaporating quicker than a drop of rain on a hot July day. "Yes, I can totally see that. What time should I meet you there?"

"Six o'clock okay?"

Glancing at the clock on the microwave, she noted it was four thirty-five. "Sounds good. I'll see you then."

Doubt encroached as she ended the call. Had she done the right thing in agreeing to have dinner with them? She had such a soft spot for Mackenzie and David, but she was walking a fine line between friendship and maternal instincts.

And then there was Crockett. Had he really been about to kiss her last night, or was she imagining things? Though the bigger question was, would she have kissed him back?

As much as she hated to admit it, yes, she would have. Simply being held in his arms had triggered a sense of longing to be loved again. But longing didn't equate to love. Yes, Crockett was a good man, but he wasn't the man for her. Even if she was willing to travel down that road again, he wasn't. His wounds had yet to heal, if they ever did, so she'd be wise to guard her heart.

By the time she made it to the restaurant, she'd convinced herself that she and Crockett had simply been caught up in the euphoria of the wedding. There was nothing romantic between them. He had no interest in getting married again, and she definitely was not interested in a man with more issues than *Time* magazine. They were friends, nothing more.

Over their meal, the kids laid out their plans for each of their parties in the barn.

"Me and my friends could play laser tag." Elbow on the table, chin in his hand, David swirled a chip through the bowl of queso. "We'd need some stuff to hide behind, though."

Crockett's fork dangled over his chicken-stuffed chile relleno. "Hay bales come to mind."

"Dad." The boy rolled his eyes. Must be taking cues from his sister.

While they waited on their tab, David looked at Paisley. "Do you have any board games?"

"Why, yes, I do." She set her napkin on the table. "My friends and I used to have game night three or four times a year. Though now that two of them are married, we don't get together much." And while she was over-the-moon happy for her friends, she missed those times.

"Do you have Monopoly?"

"I sure do. I have all the classics. Monopoly, Scrabble, Sorry!, Jenga, Yahtzee. Not to mention dominos and cards."

"Dad!" Mackenzie's face lit up. "I just had a brilliant idea." They all looked at her as she continued. "Why don't we run by the store and get some ice cream, then we can go to Paisley's to eat it and play a game."

"Mac—" Crockett glared at his daughter "—you have got to stop volunteering Paisley for things without checking with her first. She has a life, too, you know."

Her countenance fell as she peered up at Paisley with those dark eyes. "I'm sorry. I just got so excited hearing about all those games."

Paisley knew she should say no, but after being with the kids, going home to that big, empty house seemed rather unappealing at that moment. What would it hurt to play one game? And she was out of ice cream.

She looked at Crockett. "I'm down for some ice cream if you are."

He looked at her skeptically. "You sure? You were out late last night."

"I took a nap this afternoon."

He was quiet for a long moment. Probably having the same reservations about spending time with her as she was with him. Then he said, "What's your favorite ice cream flavor?"

Sitting at Paisley's kitchen table with a Sorry! game board stretched out in front of him an hour later, Crockett found himself wishing he hadn't given in to his children's whims. The fun and laughter they all enjoyed when they were with Paisley just felt so…right. And that was wrong.

This was the sort of stuff families did. Paisley wasn't family.

Still, it was impossible to ignore the positive influence she had on his kids. Selflessness was instinctive for Paisley, much the way it had been for his grandmother. Mamaw was the only woman who had ever truly loved Crockett, and she expressed it in everything she did. From the molasses cookies she'd make just for him to the Bible stories she'd share while he helped her cook to the little notes of encouragement he'd find tucked in his suitcase after he went home.

"Your turn, Dad." Arms folded atop the wooden table, Mac watched him.

He drew a card. "Five." Moving his yellow game piece, he counted off the spaces. "We should probably call it quits after this round."

"Aw." His children whined collectively.

"Why?" Mac pouted.

"Uh, because you were up till almost midnight yesterday and then had to wake up early this morning for church. After the busyness of these past few days, we could all use a good night's rest." Of course, if tonight was a repeat of last night, he wouldn't be doing much sleeping. Not when he kept thinking about how perfectly Paisley fit in his arms.

"Your dad and I have a meeting with our contractor at the castle tomorrow." Paisley picked up her water glass. "And we need to return the tables and chairs from the wedding. We should do that before our meeting with Wes."

Crockett was well aware of the meeting. However, he'd forgotten about returning stuff to the church. If either the bride's or groom's family had a trailer, he would've left it up to them. But since they didn't...

He looked across the table to Paisley. "I can handle the tables and chairs. There's no need for you to go."

"I don't expect you to load them all by yourself."

"No big deal." He lifted a shoulder. "Keeps me in shape."

"But it's time-consuming. Besides, having the reception in the barn was my idea, so I can't sit back and let you do all the heavy lifting."

"As if you sat on your laurels and did nothing. You worked your tail off."

"Doesn't matter. I'll be out at your place first thing tomorrow morning." She looked at his son. "David, it's your turn."

The last thing Crockett wanted was Paisley helping him. Not when she had a knack for making even the simplest of things fun. She'd introduced his kids to new adventures, everything from parties to picking wildflowers. Spending so much time with her had awakened something inside of Crockett. She'd given him a glimpse of the kind of life he'd once dreamed of, a life he'd planned to have with Shannon until Shannon decided he didn't meet her standards. She'd never been interested in rolling up her sleeves to help him with a project or even enjoying a board game with her kids.

"I need more ice cream." He pushed away from the table and crossed to the island.

The more he was with Paisley, the more he wanted to be with her. She made him long for the impossible. She was kind, beautiful, smart...

But she'd never be interested in a broken-down lug like him. He'd built too many walls. Even if she knocked them down, she'd see nothing but scars, ugly ones that had left him disfigured and uncertain of what love really was.

No wonder your own mother didn't want you.

Setting his bowl on the counter, he retrieved the rocky road from the freezer. As he reached for the ice cream scoop, his phone rang. He pulled it from his pocket, surprised to see his stepmother's name. Dad usually just put it on speaker so Crocket could talk to both of them.

Curious, he set the phone to his ear. "Hello, Irene."

"Crockett, I'm at the hospital with your dad."

He froze. "What happened?"

"He was working in the yard. When I went out to check on him I found him sitting on the patio, holding his chest and struggling to breathe, so I brought him to the ER. They don't think it was a heart attack, but they did find some blockages so he's going to have surgery to put in a couple of those stents."

"When?"

"They're prepping him right now."

"Now? Which hospital?"

She gave him the info.

"I'm on my way." Ending the call, he said, "Mac, David, we gotta go."

Paisley pushed out of her chair and joined him as he returned the ice cream to the freezer. Concern pinched her pretty brow. "Is something wrong?"

"My dad is in the hospital in Katy. It's his heart."

"Is Grandaddy gonna be okay?" His daughter's sad eyes peered up at him.

"I hope so, sweetness. They're going to put some stents in his heart, so that should help."

"Is there anything I can do?" Paisley wrapped an arm around David. "I could go with you in case you need me to sit with the kids, or they could stay here."

Instinct told him to say no, but at the same

time, he didn't know what to expect once he arrived at the hospital. What if they wouldn't let the kids in to see his dad? Crockett didn't like the idea of leaving them alone. But what if this was their last opportunity to see their grandfather? If something happened—

Paisley took hold of his hand. "Crockett?"

Feeling as though he'd fallen into some kind of wild dream, he looked from their joined hands to her face.

"Go start the truck. I'll grab my purse." She'd made the decision for him.

Squeezing her fingers, he said, "Thank you."

With his truck shrouded in darkness for most of the hour-and-a-half trip and the radio playing low, the kids fell asleep in the back seat while memories and what-ifs ping-ponged through Crockett's brain.

What if Dad didn't make it? Dale Devereaux had been the only constant in Crockett's life. He'd sat with Crockett when he was sick, coached Little League, watched proudly when Crockett received his high school and college diplomas, waited at the hospital when Mac and David were born, and stood by Crockett during his divorce, even though it brought back memories of his own split with Crockett's mother.

"You okay?" Out of the corner of his eye, he saw Paisley watching him.

"Just trying to convince myself that he's going to be okay."

"Angioplasty is a very common procedure."

"I know." His grip tightened on the steering wheel. "It's just…he's always been so strong and healthy. What if I lose him?"

Reaching across the console, she squeezed his forearm. "If and when that happens, you will go on, one step at a time."

One glance revealed a woman who wasn't just spouting words, but a truth she'd had to put into practice for the past five years. Her husband would have been in his prime and her son, well, Crockett had no words for that. Yet they were gone in an instant.

He laid his left hand over hers. "Paisley, I didn't mean to—"

"Don't worry. You didn't."

His kids woke up as he pulled into the hospital parking lot. He called Irene as they entered the hospital to find out where to go.

"They'll be taking him into surgery soon."

"Can I see him?"

"I believe so. Let me check." Muffled voices sifted through the line. "Yes, you can come up, Crockett."

He, Paisley and the kids took the elevator to the second floor, then Paisley stayed with the kids in the waiting room while he continued through the double doors.

Irene waited outside his father's door, her usual peaceful expression marked with concern.

He hugged the woman with short, light brown hair streaked with only the slightest hint of gray. "How is he?"

"He's stable." Her blue eyes bore into his when he released her. "Where are the kids?"

"In the waiting room with a friend."

Smiling, she said, "I'll go visit with them while you talk with your father." She patted his arm and continued down the hall.

Crockett sucked in a deep breath, uncertain of what he might find on the other side of the door. Dad had always been so strong. Invincible.

Stepping inside, the beeps of monitors and the groans of an IV machine met his ears. To his relief, though, his father didn't look too worse for wear. His color was a little off, but the oxygen tubes in his nose probably made things better.

Dad turned then, his dark eyes landing on Crockett. "'Bout time you got here."

With a weary chuckle, he approached the bed. "What's this I hear about you trying to check out on me?"

"Ah, don't you go worryin'. I'm not goin' anywhere just yet. The good Lord's still got some work to do on me."

Crockett couldn't help grinning. At least his father's sense of humor was still intact. "Guess we'd better let those doctors get you fixed up, then."

The man nodded, his smile fading as he focused on his tanned hands. "In the off chance that I'm wrong about the Lord's timing, though, will you look after Irene for me?"

Suddenly, Crockett found it hard to speak. "Of course." He had to force the words out.

"She's a special lady, Crockett. I don't know where I'd be without her." Dad and Irene met shortly after Crockett went off to college, and they married a year or so after that. She made his dad happy, which made Crockett happy.

"She's a good woman, Dad." Truth be known, he was envious of Dad and Irene. Growing old with someone you love might sound simple, but achieving it was a feat. Crockett would give anything to have what his father had.

The older man sniffed. "The best."

A woman dressed in blue scrubs came into the room. "We're ready for you, Mr. Devereaux."

Crockett held up a finger. "Can you hold on for one second while I get his wife? She's just down the hall."

"Sure."

He squeezed his father's shoulder. "I'll see you after a while."

In the waiting room, he found Irene with her arms around Mac and David, chatting with Paisley. "I told them you were on your way. They're about to take him back."

"Oh, thank you." She hugged the kids. "I'll be right back."

Taking Irene's place between Mac and David, he met Paisley's concerned gaze.

"How is he?"

"His spirits are good, and he looked better than I'd anticipated."

"Is Grandaddy going to be okay?" His boy stared up at him, uncertainty swimming in his blue eyes.

"I believe he is, son. Once they get his heart fixed up."

Returning his attention to Paisley, he said, "Thank you for coming with us. I mean, you signed on for dinner, not a trip through four counties."

"I'm happy to do it, Crockett." She shrugged. "What are friends for?"

Friends. Yeah. That's what he wanted, right? To keep Paisley at arm's length, not allow her anywhere near his battle-worn heart.

So why did he find himself suddenly hoping for more?

Chapter Twelve

Paisley couldn't recall the last time she'd been so busy. First with Mackenzie's party, then the flood, the wedding reception and the scare with Crockett's father. Thankfully, the older man was doing quite well.

She, Crockett and the kids had remained at the hospital Sunday night until Mr. Devereaux was moved to recovery. Then, after returning the items to the church and their meeting with Wes on Monday, Crockett had taken the children to see their grandfather and spend the night with Irene so he could be there when his father was released on Tuesday.

In the meantime, Paisley spoke with Molly, letting her know that the remediation had been satisfactorily completed and she had resumed packing. Though due to the flood, Wes's start date was going to be delayed. A disappointing fact, but with several homes and businesses in the area damaged, every contractor in town was scrambling to help get folks up and running as quickly as possible.

Now, as Paisley finished up breakfast at Rae's Thursday morning, she prayed she could survive her parents' visit.

They'd arrived yesterday afternoon eager to show her all of the upgrades and redecorating they'd done to their RV since their last visit, before sitting down to a dinner of grilled salmon with a heaping side of interrogation. Her parents had asked question after question, wanting to know about her day-to-day life, her friends and her plans for the future, making her wonder if they ever paid attention to anything she said when they talked on the phone.

So when Paisley slipped off to bed early last night, she'd decided to avoid round two by having breakfast out where she had friends she could call on if need be. Fortunately, her parents had behaved, thus far.

"Do you want anything else, Ms. Paisley?" Maggie, Rae's foster daughter, grinned shyly, seemingly happy to be helping. Dressed in a casual pink dress, she clasped her hands behind her back and rocked back and forth on her pink Crocs while her little brother, Max, waited behind her, looking timid, despite a sparkle in his dark brown eyes.

Paisley was thrilled that her friend had these two to keep her company. She missed the chaos of a busy household, which was only one of the reasons she loved it when Crockett and his children came to visit. She'd missed all of them this week. It had been a while since she and Crockett had gone this long without seeing each other. He'd become a good friend, though, if she didn't watch herself, he could easily become more.

"I think I'm good." She looked at her parents. "How 'bout y'all?" Reaching around the girl, Paisley tickled Max's arm. "I see you hiding back there."

The adorable five-year-old giggled.

Her mother watched the kids fondly while Dad downed the rest of his coffee.

Setting his cup on the table, he said, "We're ready when you are."

"In that case—" she looked at Maggie "—I think we are ready for our check."

The girl's smile grew wider as she handed over their bill.

"Now, that's what I call prompt service." Paisley took hold of the slip. "Thank you, Miss Maggie."

Pink tinged the girl's olive-toned cheeks as she and brother turned to leave.

"I'll take that, young lady." Dad grabbed the check. After studying it for a moment, he pulled out his wallet and left the money on the table before tugging his red Bulldogs ball cap over his white hair.

Standing, Paisley addressed her parents. "Shall we go see the castle?"

"Oh, yes." With her shoulder-length champagne-blond hair clipped to the back of her head, her mother pushed away from the table and slung her purse over her shoulder.

Temperatures were supposed to climb into the nineties today and with no air-conditioning at the castle, Paisley decided a morning visit would be best. Lord willing, the trip would finally convince her folks that she did, actually, have a life here in Bliss and a dream she desperately wanted to fulfill.

"Wow," her father said as they drove through the gates. "This really is a castle."

"Indeed, it is." Paisley wasn't about to go into the technicalities with the man. Turing off the engine, she continued. "Built by a Scotsman by the name of Angus Renwick in the late 1800s. He built it here along the river because the view reminded him of his home in Scotland."

"It's a mite warmer in Texas than it is in Scotland, though." Her father winked from the passenger seat and opened his door.

Stepping out of the vehicle, Paisley opened

the door behind her and waited for her mother to emerge. "Mama, what do you think?"

Shielding her eyes from the sun, her mother said, "I feel as though I've traveled across the pond, as they say."

"Indeed. It has a very old-world feel, which is what I'm counting on to draw people in. I mean, can you imagine getting married in a castle?"

"It would be a fairy-tale wedding, for sure," Mama said.

"The grounds are a mess due to the flood." Paisley motioned to the left and right. "But Crockett will see to it they're groomed and brought back to their original grandeur. His grandfather was the caretaker of the castle for decades, so Crockett remembers how things looked when he was a little boy."

"How much land is there?" Her father craned his neck to take in the large live oak.

"Four acres." She moved under the portico to unlock the door. "I'll take you out on the terrace later for a better view of the grounds."

Over the next hour, Paisley walked them through each and every room, detailing her and Crockett's plans before ending the tour on the terrace. "What do you think?"

Her folks exchanged a look.

"This is quite an undertaking." Her father's gaze roamed the property.

"Yes, but as I've mentioned before, the Renwicks are funding the entire project. And Crockett and I are both quite excited about preserving this unique piece of history." She watched their flat expressions as they looked out over the now blessedly low river, knowing precisely what was going through their heads.

"You think I'm making a mistake, don't you?"

"Peanut, we know that you're perfectly capable of doing anything you set your mind to. It's just—" Her father deferred to her mother.

"Don't you think it's time you came back home to Georgia, sweet pea?"

A sudden gust of warm air slapped Paisley in the face. "Why would I do that? Bliss is my home."

"Oh, now how can you say that when you don't even have a real job?" Mama all but whined. "I know Peter left you financially well off, but still, a person needs purpose, Paisley. You keep dabbling in all of these different things—" Mom gestured to the castle "— but you're simply killing time, darlin'."

"Weddings are my purpose, Mama. That's why I wanted Renwick Castle."

"Sweet pea, if you want to get back in the wedding business, why not return to Georgia where you're already established?"

"I've been gone for four years."

"People still remember Weddings by Paisley, though. Do you know how many women have lamented that you're no longer in business?"

Paisley sucked in a breath, trying not to lose her temper. "I don't want to resurrect Weddings by Paisley. I want something more. I want to benefit this community I've grown to love."

Her father's brow lifted. "This Crockett fellow wouldn't have anything to do with this, would he?"

"No. I wasn't even aware that he was interested in the castle until we met with the Renwicks' attorney. That's when we learned that the only way either of us could have access to the castle was to agree to work together, so that's what we're doing. Even if he was part of the equation, that's for me to decide."

"It's the memories, isn't it?" Lips pursed, her mother stared at her with those sad eyes she'd perfected when Paisley was a child. "You're afraid that if you return to Georgia you'll be plagued with memories of Peter and Logan."

"What? No." Would the woman ever let her move on with her life? "The memories live in here, Mama." She pointed to her heart. "They're with me no matter where I am. And I can tell you one thing—Peter would be cheering me on here, encouraging me to follow my dreams." Something her parents had never done. Instead, they always seemed to have a better plan. "I'm forty-six years old, for crying out loud. I am perfectly capable of making my own decisions. If you can't accept that, perhaps you shouldn't bother visiting me anymore."

Dad crossed his arms. "You did it again, Barbara June. You pushed her over the edge."

"Oh, you hush, Ralph." She clasped her hands against her stomach. "I'm sorry, Paisley. I didn't mean to upset you. But you know how I worry."

Paisley blew out a breath, hating that she'd allowed them to upset her so. They were her parents, after all, and only wanted the best for her. But they needed to understand that they couldn't dictate her life anymore.

"I know you do, Mama, and I'm not trying to hurt you. But I'm not a little girl anymore. You can't protect me from everything. I have to live life on my terms, and if I make a few mistakes along the way, then that's on me, too."

"I understand, baby. I won't bring it up again." Her mother hugged her, but Paisley was still unsettled. Because while she meant everything she told her mother, the woman had gotten one thing right. Paisley needed purpose. And if this castle didn't get back on track soon, she might go out of her ever-lovin' mind.

With country music blaring from the speakers, Crockett headed home from work a little early on Thursday, hoping to beat the rush at the grocery store and grab some of their fresh fried chicken for dinner. It may not be the healthiest meal, but around his house, it was definitely a crowd pleaser.

He eyed Donny Glick's hay meadow as the melody of guitar and fiddle filled the cab of his truck, thrusting his mind back to Saturday night when he was holding Paisley in his arms on the dance floor. He missed her.

He shook his head at the ridiculousness of the thought. So what if he hadn't seen her in three days? He should not be missing her. They were just friends.

When was the last time you thought about kissing one of your friends?

He roughed a hand over his face. So he enjoyed Paisley's company. Found her intriguing. That should not equate to missing her. Yet it seemed no matter how much he tried not to think about her, the desire to see her and talk with her was always there, lurking beneath the surface. Whether he wanted to admit it or not, life was just nicer when Paisley was around.

A second later, his phone rang, and her name appeared on the touch screen on his dash, sending his heart into a gallop, though he quickly discounted it. She was probably just calling to check on his dad, because it was in her nature to do stuff like that.

Hauling in a frustrated breath, he tapped the answer icon. "Well, hello there."

"Help me." The playfulness in her plea made him chuckle and put him at ease.

"Okay, I'll bite. What do you need help with?"

"My parents." Her voice was just slightly above a whisper. And judging by what sounded like birds, she was outside somewhere.

"Is something wrong?"

"Uh, if you were to ask them, they'd say I'm what's wrong."

"I'm not following you."

Her frustration crackled through the line in the form of a sigh. "They're trying to convince me to move back to Georgia."

"Why?" He tried to ignore the sliver of terror that shot through him.

"They think I'm bored here. That I have no life."

Tapping the brakes at the county line, he wished he could be there to defend her. "I would think you of all people would set them straight."

"You don't know my parents. They hear what they want to hear. I tell them I want to be in Bliss. They hear 'I can't be in Georgia because of Peter and Logan.' They're nuts, I tell ya."

He couldn't help laughing. "All right, what do

you want me to do? Pretend to be your boyfriend or something?" If only.

"Would you?"

He sobered quickly, knowing it was a role that would be all too easy to slip into. "Seriously?"

"No, that would be lying."

Unwanted disappointment washed over him.

"However, if you and the kids were to join us for dinner, even if I introduced you as my friend and explained that Mackenzie is in my Sunday school class, I have no doubt they would come to that conclusion."

His mood brightened. "So you're saying I run the risk of being interrogated by your father."

"I don't know. Maybe." She blew out a breath. "I just need a buffer. I understand if you don't want to come, but could you at least let me borrow Mackenzie and David? Of course, you'll miss out on an awesome steak dinner."

"Now you're playing dirty."

"Hey, I'm learning your weaknesses, and I'm not afraid to use them to my advantage."

Did she realize that she was quickly becoming one of his weaknesses?

"Please, Crockett. I'll bake you molasses cookies for a month."

"Wow, you really don't want to be alone with them, do you?"

"You have no idea." He'd missed their playful banter.

"All right, we'll be there. But only because it'll be fun to watch you squirm."

There was a long pause. Then, "Why would I squirm?"

"Guess you'll just have to wait and find out."

"Crockett Devereaux."

He busted out laughing. He liked it when she got riled up. "Do you want us to come or not?"

She heaved a sigh. "Yes."

"Okay. We'll see you at six."

Ending the call, he sat a little taller as he changed directions to head for home. The fact that Paisley had asked him and the kids to come to her aid did strange things to his psyche. She could have asked one of her friends, but she'd called him. And something about that made him very happy.

He pulled into his driveway a short time later, eager to tell the kids. They were going to be ecstatic. They'd missed Paisley, too.

After parking his truck, he headed inside.

"Oh, good. You're home." Ashley stood from her spot next to David on the couch. "David's not feeling well."

"What's the matter, bud?" He crossed to join them, concern and disappointment warring inside of him.

"He's running a slight fever," the sitter said.

"My head and my tummy don't feel so good either," his boy added.

"When did it start?" Crockett eyed Ashley.

"Just in the last hour or so. That's why I didn't call. I knew you'd be home soon."

"No, you're fine." He crouched beside his boy. "I'm sorry you're not feeling well." For more than one reason. He couldn't leave his son, but it meant he was going to have to disappoint Paisley.

"Will you sit with me?"

"I sure will. Just give me a minute." Standing, he turned to face Ashley. "Would you mind staying with him while I make a phone call? I won't be long."

"No problem."

Returning to the front porch, he checked his watch before dialing. It was already five. Paisley probably had most of the meal going already.

She picked up on the third ring, "Hello."

"Paisley." He rubbed the back of his neck. "I'm afraid I have some bad news."

"Is something wrong?"

"Yeah. I just got home." He saw Mac emerge from the horse barn. Spotting him, she waved. "David's sick, so it looks like we're not going to be able to make it for dinner." He waved to his daughter.

"Poor guy. I'm so sorry to hear that." Noises

in the background told him she was in the middle of preparing dinner, a dinner he'd give anything to be there for. "Any idea what's wrong?"

"Sitter says he has a low-grade fever. He says he feels bad."

"Sounds like he picked up a bug somewhere. At least, I hope that's all it is."

"Paislcy, I'm really sorry to back out on you like this."

"Crockett, your kids come first. I understand that. I just hate that David is sick. Give him a hug for me and tell him I said to get well soon." The woman had a heart as big as the Grand Canyon.

"I'll do that."

Ending the call, he stared out over the pasture, feeling kinda sick himself. Though it had been short-lived, he'd been really looking forward to seeing Paisley tonight. He'd wanted to ride in there and play the hero, saving her from whatever was bothering her. Instead, he'd disappointed her.

You're no hero.

He hung his head. No, he wasn't. Not by a long shot. And he'd never be worthy of a woman like Paisley.

Chapter Thirteen

Paisley could finally breathe again. Her parents had pulled away in their RV a little after eight Friday morning with a promise to support her as she eased back into the wedding business in Bliss and to stop thinking of her as perpetually in mourning. Actually, their dinner last night had gone quite well, despite it being just the three of them. Perhaps they'd finally realized that she was stronger than they believed her to be.

Of course, as soon as they were gone, her thoughts turned to David. He was such a happy-go-lucky boy. Just the notion of him being sick made her sad, so she'd given Crockett a call to see how he was doing. He was better, but Crockett had decided to stay home with him today. That didn't mean he wasn't in demand, though. He'd had to cut their call short to take another from the office.

It wasn't until after she hung up that she decided to make a batch of chicken soup along with some molasses cookies. Because even though Crockett wasn't able to make it last night, he'd still been willing.

Pulling into Crockett's drive just before noon, she tried to convince herself that she was simply providing some nourishment for a sick little boy and that the decision to make the soup and cookies had nothing to do with wanting to spend time with Crockett. Yet no matter how many times she tried, she failed. She and Crockett had, indeed, become friends, but all too often lately she found herself wondering if they could be more. Not only did she wonder, sometimes she hoped.

Somewhere along the way, she'd stopped thinking of Crockett as the enemy and started entertaining a plethora of what-ifs. He wasn't the heartless person she'd once imagined him to be. He was kind, caring, an adoring father... And they'd worked so well together on Samantha's wedding. Where one was weak, the other was strong.

But he doesn't want another relationship. He has trust issues.

Then why had he almost kissed her?

You don't know that. And you cannot hang your hat on a man who's been wounded by love.

Blowing out an annoyed breath, she parked

her SUV, gathered up the food and knocked on the door.

Moments later, it opened, and Crockett stood on the other side looking more handsome than a man had a right to in jeans and a gray Devereaux Sand and Gravel T-shirt.

"I wasn't expecting to see you." He shifted from one bare foot to the other, looking rather unhappy. As though he didn't want her there.

Now she wished she'd told him she was coming. "I, uh, I made some chicken soup for David. There's enough for everyone, of course." Lifting her chin a notch, she added, "And there are some molasses cookies, too."

His narrowed gaze slammed into hers. "You shouldn't have done that." His voice was harsh, and he had a scowl to match.

While she had no idea why he was upset, she refused to react in kind. She squared her shoulders. "I told you I would make you cookies. It wasn't your fault you weren't able to come by last night. Consider it your reward for being willing."

He stared at her for a long moment, his jaw pulsating. Was he contemplating sending her away, cookies and all?

Finally, his shoulders became less rigid, and the hard lines on his face eased as he took the containers from her. "Thank you. Come on in."

David was on the sofa in the living room,

watching a cartoon. His face lit up when he saw her, erasing any remorse she had following his father's less-than-welcome reception.

"Hey there, darlin'." She crossed to kneel beside him. "How are you feeling?"

Head propped on a pillow, he said, "Dad says my fever's gone, but I still feel kinda yucky."

She stroked the hair from his brow. "Yucky is never fun, is it?"

"I feel better now that you're here."

"I'm happy to see you, too." Smiling, she patted his arm. "I brought you some soup."

"Thanks. If you made it, I know it's going to be good."

"You are such a sweetie." More than she could say for his father at that moment. Why was he acting like the old Crockett? The one who couldn't stand to be in the same room with her.

She pushed to her feet, eyeing him in the kitchen. "Where's Mackenzie?"

"Working." Crockett looked everywhere but at her.

Continuing toward the island, Paisley said, "I had promised her a trip to the city for some shopping. I thought next Saturday might be a good time for that, if it's all right with you."

"How long will you be gone?" He loaded a coffee mug and a glass into the dishwasher without ever looking her way.

"Most of the day, I'm sure."

He concentrated on loading a couple of bowls and spoons, seemingly mulling over his decision. "She's been looking forward to that trip ever since you first mentioned it. We've got nothing planned, so yeah, I guess that'll be all right."

Paisley couldn't help smiling. "Thank you. I promise to keep her safe and sound."

He nodded but still didn't look at her as he closed the door on the dishwasher. What was up with him today? Perhaps something had happened with his father.

"How is your father doing?"

"He's fine."

Why were his answers so clipped? Just the facts, ma'am, as though he were merely enduring their conversation.

"Is something wrong, Crockett?" Perhaps she should leave. He obviously didn't want her around. A thought that, surprisingly, made her sad.

A racket sounded from the laundry/mudroom off of the kitchen, drawing their attention. A second later, Mackenzie appeared, wearing a dust-covered blue tank top over faded jeans, her sock feet evidence that she'd removed her boots in the mudroom.

Her smile was instantaneous when she spotted Paisley. She continued toward her. "What are you doing here?"

Paisley slipped an arm around her shoulders for a sideways hug. The girl smelled of horse and bubble gum. "Checking on your brother."

"She brought soup and cookies, too," David hollered from the sofa. And here Paisley thought he was engrossed in his television show.

"What kind?" Mackenzie's eyes widened.

"Chicken soup, because of its healing properties, and molasses cookies, just because." She glanced toward the kitchen to see Crockett watching them, his expression pensive.

The ringtone on his phone sounded. He eyed the device on the counter before picking it up. "Yeah." His brow puckered as he moved from the kitchen into the front room that he used for an office.

Paisley watched him go, wishing she knew what had gotten into him.

Returning her attention to Mackenzie, she pulled a piece of hay from the girl's ponytail. "Your father and I have been talking. What would you think about making that run into the city with me a week from tomorrow?"

The girl let out a high-pitched squeal and began bouncing around. "Yes! Yes! Yes!"

Crockett poked his head around the corner. "Mac! Please, I'm on the phone."

His daughter smiled sheepishly. "We are going to have so much fun," she whispered. "I really want to find some new sandals and, maybe, a sundress for church."

"Well, we'll have all day to look."

"I need to hurry up and eat lunch then, so I can get back out to the barn and earn some more money."

Paisley couldn't help laughing. "A little motivation never hurts."

"Can I have some soup?"

"Sure, I brought plenty. It's in that pot over there on the stove." She pointed.

While Mackenzie helped herself, Paisley went to check on David. "Do you feel up to eating a little something, or would you prefer to wait?"

His blue eyes met hers. "Can I have just a little bit?"

"You certainly may. I'll be right back."

Paisley addressed Mackenzie as the girl settled in at the table. "Can you point me to the bowls?"

"That cupboard right there." She pointed to the right of the stove.

"Thank you, darlin'."

Bowl in hand, she ladled the soup as Crockett returned, rubbing the back of his neck. A sure indication something was troubling him.

"What's wrong?"

Shaking his head, he said, "I really hate to ask you this, but is there any chance you could watch the kids for me? I completely forgot that

I'd scheduled an appointment with a project manager today. Now he's at the plant and I'm not."

"Oh, that's not good. Yes, of course I can watch them. How long do you think you'll be?"

"No idea. But it could be a while."

"No problem." She set the ladle on the spoon rest beside the stove. "You go do what you need to do. The kids and I will be fine."

"You're sure you don't mind?"

Replacing the lid, she said, "Not at all. What little is left to pack-up at the castle can wait."

He watched her for a long moment. "I'll be back as soon as the meeting is over. Then you'll be free to leave whenever you like."

"I'm not worried. Take as long as you need."

A tentative smile played at his lips. "Thank you."

She watched him pull out of the drive a few minutes later, still curious as to why he'd been so distant earlier when everything seemed fine when they'd talked yesterday. And why did that distance bother her so much?

Unfortunately, she knew the answer to that question. Her feelings for Crockett were teetering between friendship and something more. And that scared her. She'd known love in its most precious form. Yet, in a flash, it was gone. Did she want to risk going through that again?

Better to have loved and lost than to never have loved at all.

Those words had rolled off her tongue so easily when she accused her friend Christa of being afraid to love for fear of losing. Back then, though, Paisley never imagined finding someone who would make her want to open her heart. Now she wasn't sure what to do.

She'd loved Peter and Logan with her whole heart, only to be crushed when they died. There were no certainties in life. She cared a great deal for Crockett, but allowing herself to love that way again? That was positively terrifying.

"Crockett, I apologize for takin' you away from your boy." Hank Remington with Glendale Homes stood from the chair opposite Crockett. The builder was in the development phase of a master planned community southwest of Houston and was looking at Devereaux Sand and Gravel to provide the base material for new streets.

"No apologies necessary." Standing, Crockett rounded his desk. "This is on me. I failed to notify you."

"I'm a firm believer that family comes first. And having a sick young'un is never convenient, so I'm glad we were able to work things out."

Thanks to Paisley. If she hadn't been so gracious as to stay with Mac and David he didn't know what he would have done. But he would have stood a good chance of losing Glendale's business.

Crockett reached for the door. "Thank you for understanding."

They continued into the main part of the building.

Hank set his straw cowboy hat atop his head. "I'm going to get on out of here so you can check on your boy."

Crockett followed him out the door where the rumble of truck engines and heavy machinery had him raising his voice. "I'll get those numbers worked up and have them to you by Tuesday."

The two shook hands and, as Hank departed, Crockett returned to the metal building that housed the offices.

Pausing near his assistant's desk, he said, "Any messages, Kelly?"

The mother of three in her late thirties looked up at him. "No, sir. But then, it's almost the end of the day. It's a Friday and school's out for summer, so a lot of people are probably knocking off early."

He checked his watch, surprised to see that it was four thirty. "I had no idea it was so late."

"Does that mean you had a good meeting?" Kelly smiled and pushed her keyboard aside.

"I think so. We'll know better after I send them my proposal. For now, though, I need to get on home to David." Of course, Paisley would be there, too. And after the way Crockett behaved this morning, that might not be a good thing. He reached around the corner and turned off the light in his office before closing the door. "Enjoy your weekend, Kelly."

"You, too. I hope David feels better soon."

He pushed open the main door. "Me, too."

Outside, the late afternoon sun blazed overhead as he hurried to his truck amid the reverberations of the plant, kicking himself for being so cold to Paisley. She was just being her usual kind self, bringing food and checking on his son, not to mention offering to take his daughter shopping. Yet Crockett had rebuffed her at every turn. How was he going to face her again?

Climbing into his truck, he thought back to Sunday night and how readily she'd offered to go with them to the hospital, despite the long drive and having been up late the night before. Paisley routinely gave of herself without expecting anything in return. He wasn't used to that. Shannon took and took and took. Any giving on her part came only when it benefitted her. The two women couldn't be more different. At least he wouldn't have to worry about Paisley backing out on Mac.

So why do you keep comparing them?

Because he was an idiot.

He turned onto the county road and let go a sigh. It seemed that whenever he erected a new wall to keep Paisley away from his heart, she found a way to knock it down. Aside from his grandmother and Irene, he'd never encountered someone so selfless. Not only did it blow him away, it made it difficult to keep his feelings in check. Paisley made him want to let her in, but then the what-ifs would take over. What if she decided he wasn't enough? Or that caring about him was a mistake? Or he wasn't worth the effort?

What if she said yes?

"God, what am I doing?" His prayer filled the cab of his pickup. "Why am I so conflicted when it comes to Paisley?"

I don't know where I'd be without her.

His father's words replayed in his mind. Crockett had been surprised when he'd learned his dad was dating Irene. How had Dad managed to open himself up to love again after what Crockett's mother had done to him, though? Then again, Dad had grown up with a loving mother who'd wanted him.

Pulling up to his house twenty minutes later, he killed the engine and drew in a bolstering breath. *Lord, help me. I don't know what to think.*

After exiting his truck, he walked through the front door to a mixture of tantalizing aromas. Sweet mingled with spicy, awakening his appetite. Then he realized he'd never eaten lunch. And the granola bar he'd eaten on his way to the plant was long gone.

Laughter met his ears as he moved into the living room, drawing his attention to the kitchen table where Paisley and his children sat playing a game of some sort. The scene had him stopping in his tracks, not to mention stealing his breath.

This was the image that had lived in his mind since he was a little boy. The scene he'd always dreamed of coming home to but had always been out of his reach. The only difference was that in his mind the beautiful woman waiting had been his wife. He no longer had one of those. Even when he had, this never existed. Matter of fact, toward the end, it was a nanny he'd come home to while Shannon was off doing her own thing.

"Hey, Dad." Spotting him first, Mac waved before returning her focus to their game.

"Hi, Dad." David simply waved without ever looking at Crockett.

"Well, hello." Paisley pushed out of her chair and stood. Moving between the table and island, she said, "How was your meeting?"

He cleared his throat. "Much longer than I anticipated. Sorry I'm so late."

She smiled up at him. "You're not late. Dinner is still in the oven."

"Whatever it is smells delicious."

"It's chicken spaghetti. I hope you don't mind. The kids said they liked it."

He rubbed the back of his neck, feeling rather humbled. "No, not at all. I wasn't aware that I had one of those in the freezer. I must have grabbed that box instead of the lasagna."

Looking at him curiously, she said, "This chicken spaghetti didn't come out of a box. We made it. You had some leftover chicken in the refrigerator, cheese, spaghetti." She lifted a shoulder. "The kids helped me make it."

And he had no doubt that they enjoyed every minute of it. "How's David doing?"

"Fine. He ate two bowls of soup for lunch, not to mention nibbled while we were cooking, so his appetite has definitely returned, and he's had no fever."

Crockett let go a sigh of relief. "That's good to hear. I was hoping to visit my dad this weekend, but not if David's sick."

"Barring anything unforeseen, he should be fine."

"So, what do I smell that's sweet?"

"Peach cobbler. You had some frozen peaches."

He shook his head. "You never cease to amaze me, you know that?"

"Good. Keeps you on your toes."

A timer beeped.

"That would be the casserole." Paisley returned to the kitchen while Crockett went to greet his kids.

"What are y'all playing?"

"Yahtzee." His boy grinned. "I won the first round."

Not to be outdone, Mac added, "But I'm winning this one."

Glancing toward the kitchen, he couldn't help noticing that everything was spotless. The countertops were not only visible, they gleamed. Papers that had been scattered were neatly stacked, odds and ends that always seemed to find their way into the kitchen were gone, the refrigerator was void of fingerprints, even the sink had been scrubbed. And the picture-perfect cobbler waited beside the stove while the still-bubbling chicken spaghetti rested atop one of the burners.

God, if You're trying to make a point, I think I got it.

"All right, you two." Addressing his children, Paisley held her arms wide. "Give me hugs."

"You're leaving?" Mac looked horrified at the notion.

Wrapping her arms around his son, Paisley said, "I don't want to wear out my welcome."

Crockett didn't know if her phrasing was

aimed at him, but he did know that he'd done nothing to make her feel welcome when she'd arrived late this morning. On the contrary, he'd given her the cold shoulder. And he'd been kicking himself ever since.

As she gathered up the now-empty pot she'd brought the soup in, he stepped in front of her. "Please stay."

She looked up at him. "I'm sorry I intruded on you earlier."

He couldn't believe she was actually apologizing to him. "You have nothing to be sorry for, Paisley. I was the one who behaved badly. I was—" *afraid that I'm falling for you.* "If you have to go, I understand. But just know that I don't want you to. I want you to stay, too."

Her sapphire eyes searched his. "I'm sorry. I just can't."

Chapter Fourteen

Crockett had no one to blame but himself. If he hadn't been so rude to Paisley when she'd shown up unexpectedly yesterday, she might have stayed for dinner last night, allowing him to enjoy her company and bask in how good being with her made him feel.

But no. Thanks to his stupidity, she'd gone, leaving him to grouse over the great meal she'd prepared. What was that Bible verse that equated kindness with heaping hot coals on someone? Yeah, that's what it was like. And he didn't care for it one bit.

Nope, he couldn't fault Paisley. He wouldn't want to hang out with someone who acted as though they didn't want him around either.

Isn't that what you were trying to achieve, though? Keeping her away?

At this point, he had no idea what he wanted. All he knew was that he had to find some way to make amends because if nothing else, they were still business partners. He just wasn't sure if that was enough anymore.

Pulling up to Dad and Irene's brick single-story house northwest of Houston, he hoped the man might have some sage advice. No one knew Crockett better than his dad. He'd seen every scar on Crockett's battle-worn heart, and he loved him anyway.

By the time Crockett and the kids emerged from the truck, a smiling Irene was waiting on the porch. "I'm so happy to see you." Her arms were wide as the kids hurried to greet her. Since Shannon's parents had relinquished their role as grandparents when she decided she no longer wanted to be a mother, Irene was the only grandmother Mac and David had. And since Irene never had any children of her own, she reveled in the fact that they were all hers.

"Where's Grandaddy?" David peered up at the woman.

Lovingly brushing the hair off his brow, she said, "He's in the living room, waiting for someone to play dominoes with him."

"I can do that." The happy boy scurried past her and disappeared into the house.

"Wait for me!" Mackenzie snagged a quick hug before following her brother.

"How's it going, Irene?" Under a clear blue

sky, Crockett strode onto the porch and hugged the woman, dwarfing her petite five-foot-four frame.

"It's going well." She smiled up at him now. "The doctor says your father is doing great and should be back to his regular activities soon."

"That's good to hear. But what I want to know is how you're holding up."

"Oh, don't worry about me." She waved a hand. "I'm right as rain."

He couldn't help laughing. "Considering the flooding rains we had a couple of weeks ago, I'm not sure if that's a good thing or not."

Patting his back, she said, "It's all good. By the way, I enjoyed meeting your friend Paisley. I just wish it had been under different circumstances. She seems like a lovely person."

"She is." Inside and out. "Reminds me of you, actually."

"I will consider that a compliment." With a knowing look, she added, "Paisley appears quite taken with you and the kids, too."

"The kids, yes. Me? I'm not so sure."

"Do I detect a hint of disappointment?"

"You know, Irene, that's what I've been trying to figure out myself."

Her blue eyes watched him intently. She knew his issues almost as well as his father because the two of them shared everything. Unlike his marriage, which had been full of secrets he'd been too blind to see.

"Don't allow the decisions of others to define you, Crockett. What they think doesn't matter. It's how God views you that matters, and the blood of Jesus makes you perfect in His sight."

His smile was instantaneous. Irene had always been the ultimate encourager. She made him wish she'd been a part of their lives while he was growing up.

Slipping an arm over her shoulders, he guided her into the house. "How did you know I needed that reminder?"

"I was a schoolteacher. I've learned to be very perceptive."

After a simple lunch of sandwiches, chips and fresh fruit, Irene invited the kids to help her make cookies while Crockett and his father migrated to the patio with their iced tea. He appreciated how his stepmother always saw to it that Crockett had some time alone with his father. Today she probably expected he needed it.

"You look much better." Crockett set his cup on the table before settling into one of the cushioned chairs on the covered patio, thankful for the ceiling fan rapidly moving the humid air.

"Wish I could say the same about you."

He shot his father a look that held as much confusion as it did annoyance.

"You're lookin' a little peaked, son. Wouldn't have anything to do with that Paisley gal Irene said was with you at the hospital, would it?"

Crockett shook his head. "Irene sure seems to have read a lot into Paisley bein' with me."

"Well, when was the last time you showed up anywhere with a woman at your side?" Given Shannon's propensity for roaming, probably a lot longer than five years.

Letting go a sigh, Crockett leaned back in his chair and clasped his hands behind his neck. "Dad, how did you work up the courage to trust your heart to another woman?"

The man stared into his glass for a long moment as a mourning dove cooed a woeful melody nearby. "It wasn't easy, I can tell you that. 'Course, I was my own worst enemy." His dark gaze met Crockett's. "Sometimes it's easier to hide away and wallow in the pain than to move on."

"You're telling me. Just the thought of moving on—not to mention, possibly getting hurt again—is enough to scare me."

"I'm ashamed to say that I allowed myself to become a victim of someone else's actions."

"And yet you still married again?"

Dad's expression became stern. "Crockett, your mama leaving didn't make me a victim."

Crockett eyed a squirrel shimmying along the grayed fence pickets. "That's not how I see it."

"Well, then you'd be wrong." Leaning closer, his father continued. "I became a victim when I accepted the responsibility for your mama leaving."

Crockett straightened and reached for his tea. "I guess that's one way to look at it." He took a sip.

"By blaming your mother for my misery, I was giving her control over my life instead of God."

Just the way Crockett blamed Shannon. Except he blamed his mother, too.

He shifted in his seat. "That's rather convicting."

"Yes, it is. And it took me a long time to realize what I was doing. But soon as I did, I asked the good Lord to forgive me." Retrieving his glass, he leaned back in his seat. "'Course then I had to forgive your mother."

Crockett nearly spewed his tea. "How could you forgive her after what she did to us?"

"Son, with God, all things are possible. And when He asks you to do somethin', you can either wrestle with Him or give in. I wasn't the reason your mother left, she was. That's on her, not me."

Wrapping his brain around the concept of forgiving his mother and Shannon was a challenge Crockett wasn't sure he could meet.

"Okay, but what about Irene? I mean, you could have done all of that and still not pursued her."

A grin split his father's face. "Sometimes God presents us with an offer that's too good to refuse. Irene is one special gal. It was easier to love her than to try not to."

Thoughts of Paisley played across Crockett's mind. The way she'd cared for Mac and David the night of the storm. The strength of character it took to move forward after losing her husband and son. That alone was enough to put him to shame.

"Believe it or not, that I understand."

His father's smile grew wider. "In that case, there might be hope for you yet, my boy."

"I think we should celebrate."

Standing in the entry hall of the castle Wednesday afternoon, Paisley looked at Crockett, wondering what had gotten into him. He'd been different lately. Happier, maybe. More carefree. Definitely not as uptight.

He'd been at the castle with her for a few hours each day this week, helping her with the packing since the movers were due to arrive today. Then he'd been there since first thing this morning to help her oversee the process. She hadn't expected that. Or his cheery disposition. That alone had her reconsidering her determination to keep things strictly business.

Now as the movers pulled away just after four, he thought they should celebrate. Since when was that word even in his vocabulary?

Still skeptical, she looked at him. "And how do you propose we do that?"

"I've been promising the kids we'd go for an evening ride. And since it's not as hot today, I thought tonight would be a good time. If you were to go with us, it would be downright perfect."

Her gaze locked with his. The look in his eyes, the timbre of his voice made her feel as though he truly wanted her to join them. Of course, experience had taught her his mood could turn on a dime.

"I assume you're talking about horseback riding."

"Yes. Sorry, I should have clarified. Do you know how to ride?"

"It's been years, but yes. I even took lessons once upon a time." Riding with Crockett and the kids would probably be lovely, much the way things had been when they were prepping the barn for Samantha's wedding reception. But then, for whatever reason, Crockett had become distant, seemingly slamming the door in her face. At least that's how it had felt. Last Friday at his house, he'd definitely shut her out, and it hurt. She didn't want to hurt anymore. She'd had more than her fair share.

"Paisley?"

She looked up to see him approach.

He stopped mere inches from her. "I'm sorry for the way I treated you Friday. I like being with you, perhaps a little too much, and I got into my head. I was afraid of my feelings for you." His fingers reached for hers. "I don't want to be afraid anymore."

A lightness came over Paisley, and she felt almost giddy.

Unable to contain her smile, she said, "Let's go ride some horses."

She was glad she had her own vehicle because she needed the twenty-minute drive to settle her flailing nerves. She felt like she was in junior high again and had just found out that the boy she'd been crushing on liked her back. She wanted to squeal. And since she was alone in her SUV, she did just that.

Crockett wasn't the only one who was afraid, though. What if fear had him taking a step back once again?

Then she'd just have to coax him back to reality and let him know she would never intentionally hurt him.

Once she arrived at the ranch, she tried to

maintain her usual calm and collected persona. Crockett had called the kids to let them know they'd be riding, so they were ready and waiting.

"I'm so excited you're going with us." Mackenzie bounded alongside her on the way to the horse barn.

"Me, too." Her gaze shifted from Mackenzie to her father, who happened to be watching them. When he saw Paisley look his way, he shot her a wink that had her heart racing again.

The late afternoon air held a hint of a breeze as they set out across the pasture a short time later.

"You look like a natural up there." Beside her, Crockett smiled at her from atop his sorrel steed.

"I think Cupcake and I are going to get along just fine." She patted her palomino's neck.

A smiling David moved to her right. "You should ride with us more often, Ms. Paisley."

At the moment, she wouldn't mind that at all.

They moved at a leisurely pace until they reached the edge of the pasture where Crockett dismounted to open a gate, allowing Paisley and the kids to pass through before rejoining them.

As they continued on, the woods closed in, funneling them onto a narrow path. Mackenzie took the lead, followed by David and Paisley while Crockett brought up the rear.

The horses picked their way along a slowly descending, sandy path flanked with mighty oaks, spindly cedars, pines and yaupon.

Sunlight flickered through the bright green leaves, and Paisley drew in a deep breath of earthy air. "Is it me, or does it feel like it's getting cooler?" She glanced over her shoulder at Crockett.

"It's not your imagination. There's a creek up ahead that keeps this area a few degrees cooler."

"Creek?" Still holding the reins, she twisted in her saddle to look at him. "You know we had a lot of rain, right?"

"Don't worry. Carlos checked it out the other day. It's a little wider than usual, but no roaring rapids, so we'll be fine."

He was right, of course, and a short time later, the horses splashed across the shallow creek that snaked through the trees and underbrush.

"Dad," David hollered back as the horses picked their way up the trail, "can we go fishing?"

"I don't see why not."

Paisley hadn't seen any fishing poles, but she had a feeling Crockett somehow had things covered.

Several minutes later, they veered off the trail, ducking as they passed under some low-hanging pine boughs before emerging onto the banks of a pond that was tucked in the middle of the woods.

"This is beautiful," she said as Crockett appeared at her side.

"It's a nice change of pace." He held on to Cupcake's reins as Paisley climbed down.

Looking up at him, she felt her heart flutter. "As is this ride. Thank you for inviting me."

"You're welcome."

When she turned around, she saw each of the kids holding fishing poles. "Where did you get those?"

"They were on our saddles," said Mackenzie. "In these." She held up a small bag.

"Ever hear of collapsible fishing poles?" Crockett's whisper made her shiver.

Rubbing her arms, she said, "No, but then you've probably never heard of pate a choux, so we're even."

"At least collapsible fishing pole kinda gives things away. I have no clue what you're talking about."

She couldn't help laughing. "As it should be."

While the kids cast their lines, Crockett took hold of Paisley's hand. "Come with me."

She looked from the kids to him and back again. "Are you sure they'll be okay?"

"We'll still be within earshot."

Hand in hand, they picked their way into the woods until they came to a sprawling live oak.

Taking in the tree's wide-reaching limbs, she said, "I can't get over how peaceful it is out here."

"It's even better when you're here."

She turned to find Crockett's gaze fixed on her. Staring into his eyes, her mouth went dry and her heart couldn't seem to decide if it should stand still or beat a rhythm like a mighty bass drum. And when his calloused hand cupped her cheek, she thought she might melt into a puddle.

Leaning into his touch, she closed her eyes, savoring his presence and the aroma of soap, horse and hard work. It seemed like a lifetime since she'd felt this way. Then Crockett's lips touched hers and she found herself caught up in a heady whirlwind of emotions. She was falling in love with Crockett, of that she had no doubt.

She wrapped her arms around him, not wanting the moment to end.

"Got one." David's voice carried on the gentle breeze.

Crockett reluctantly pulled away, leaving her longing for more. "That boy of mine has terrible timing."

She laughed softly as he wrapped his arms around her and held her close, making her feel treasured and wanted. A second later, he kissed her forehead and stepped away.

"Guess I'd better go help him." He held out his hand.

"It's okay, you go on. I'll catch up." She needed a moment to rein herself in. That kiss had been as unexpected as it was delightful. Yet as she willed the heat away from her cheeks, another thought wormed its way into her mind, eating away at her euphoria.

Falling in love meant opening herself up to the possibility of loss. And she didn't want to go through that ever again.

Chapter Fifteen

"You're sure you want to do this?"

Decked out in a hard hat, goggles and gloves, Paisley wielded a sledgehammer in the kitchen of the castle the next morning, eyeing Crockett. "We all agreed that the kitchen is a gut job. And since it's going to be a while before Wes can get his crew in here, why not save them some time by doing what we can?"

Crockett's sly grin made her heart quiver. Or, perhaps, it was the memory of his kiss that kept replaying in her mind. "You think this is going to be easy, don't you?"

"Maybe. Not really. But I bet it'll be fun."

"I don't think we'll need the sledgehammer, though."

She frowned. "Why not?"

"These cabinets are made of some quality oak. We should try to salvage them and, if the Renwicks agree, which I'm sure they will, they can be donated and reused."

"That's actually a really good idea."

He puffed his chest out, further straining the fabric of his T-shirt. "It happens on occasion."

More than occasionally. His idea to take the kids horseback riding ranked right up there, too.

"So, instead of using this— " he took the sledgehammer from her and set it against the wall "—we're going to use this." He held up a drill.

"Why do guys always find a way to use power tools?"

"Because they're faster. Now let's get to work."

They did just that and by the time lunch rolled around, they'd removed half of the upper cabinets and moved them into the dining room. They were heavy and cumbersome, not to mention a little greasy, but at least they were making progress.

"I think I'm ready for a break." Crockett swept his forearm across his brow.

Looking at the now-empty spaces, she said, "I believe we've earned it."

Her phone buzzed in her back pocket. Noting the number, she tugged off her gloves to answer it. "Hello."

"Hi, Paisley. This is Sandy over at The Stitch House. I've got your order ready to go."

"That's wonderful! I can't wait to see them." She'd dropped off a diaper bag, blanket and bib to be embroidered with the name of Laurel's baby boy.

"All right, then. We're here till five."

"You know, we're about to break for lunch, so I'm just going to run over there right now." It was only a twenty-five-minute drive to the neighboring town of Bluebird.

"All righty, then. We'll be lookin' for you."

Crockett eyed her as she ended the call. "Sounds like I'm on my own for lunch."

"I thought you said you needed to run by the plant."

"I do." Taking a step closer, he slipped an arm around her waist. "That's not near as enticing as having lunch with you, though." He dropped a quick kiss on her lips before releasing her.

"Shall we meet back here, or will you be staying at the plant?"

"I'll have to call and let you know."

Removing her hat and goggles, she said, "All right. I will see you later."

She pulled away from the castle and drove west of Bliss to hop on the state highway. As she sped past ranches and the occasional shop, Crockett was never far from her mind. She still couldn't get over how his attitude had changed this past week. Had he really been able to shake off his fears?

After exiting, she made her way into Bluebird proper until she reached Main Street. Moments later, she parked in front of The Stitch House, a quaint little shop that catered to enthusiasts of any type of needlework, whether it was sewing, embroidery, knitting or crochet.

Pushing through the door of the narrow building, her eye was immediately drawn to the colorful skeins of yarn covering the back wall. Walls to the right and left held bolts of fabric in an array of colors and patterns.

"Hi, Paisley." Sandy poked her head out of the back room. "Let me grab your order." In no time, she reappeared and laid the items on one of three wooden tables that ran down the middle of the store.

"These are so cute." Paisley fingered the navy lettering on the gray diaper bag, her gaze taking in the light gray microfiber blanket and the bib embroidered with the identical color and whimsical font. "Laurel is going to love these."

After paying, she returned to her SUV and headed back to Bliss, her heart set on stopping by Rae's for some lunch so that she could show her friend the items.

She merged onto the highway, thinking that embroidered fleece blankets might make nice gifts for David and Mackenzie, too. She'd have to keep her eye out for something that would suit their personalities.

Cruising along in the right-hand lane, she noticed the semi coming up on her left in her side mirror. And as she glanced at her rearview mirror, she saw a pickup truck bearing down on her bumper.

She huffed out a breath. "Mister, if you think that's going to make me speed up, you're mistaken."

As soon as the semi had inched far enough forward, the pickup whipped into the other lane, practically clinging to the semi's rear end.

The whole scene irritated Paisley. Just because the fellow in the pickup was in a hurry didn't mean he had to jeopardize the safety of others.

She eased up on the gas, allowing the semi to fully pass. It'd barely cleared her vehicle when the pickup zoomed past her, aiming for the small gap between her and the semi.

Anxiety swelled in her chest, her grip tightening on the wheel. She took her foot off the gas, but it was too late. The pickup plowed ahead, clipping her bumper in the process.

Her heartbeat thundered in her ears as her SUV lurched to the right. She eyed the steep grade beyond the shoulder and overcorrected. Left then right.

When she finally came to a stop at the side of the road, she put the vehicle into Park and dropped her head against the steering wheel. Terror pulsed through her veins as images of Peter and Logan's wreckage played through her mind.

That could have been her.

Her phone rang, jarring her from the turmoil. She looked at the screen on her dash to see Mackenzie's name. Before she could think better of it, she fingered the answer button.

"H-hello."

"It's Mackenzie. I just wanted to call and tell you how excited I am about our trip Saturday. What time should I be ready?"

Their shopping trip to the city.

Paisley stared at the cars whizzing past her. What if Mackenzie had been with her? What if something happened Saturday? She'd promised Crockett she'd keep Mackenzie safe and sound, but what if she couldn't? Peter hadn't been able to protect Logan.

Tears pricked the backs of her eyes. She couldn't do it. Couldn't put Mackenzie at risk like that. No matter how much it hurt her.

"Ms. Paisley?"

She sucked in a breath. "I—I'm here. Um, I'm afraid we're going to have to cancel our trip. Something's come up, and I'm not going to be able to go."

"Oh. That's okay. We can go another time."

Paisley squeezed her eyes shut. "I don't know. Things will be getting busy at the castle soon. I don't think I'll be able to break away."

"Oh." The girl was quiet for a long while. Finally, "I guess I'll talk to you later, then." Her voice cracked as she said goodbye, piercing Paisley's heart.

She'd disappointed Crockett's daughter the same way Crockett's ex-wife had. But Paisley would rather see Mackenzie alive and well and upset with her rather than see Crockett go through what Paisley had endured, even if he ended up hating her, too.

Again, the images of Peter's crash blazed through her mind. She recalled the hopelessness she'd felt in the weeks and months that followed. She never wanted to feel that way again.

But sitting there on the side of the road, fear slowly ebbing, she was reminded that life held no guarantees and love did not conquer all. Sometimes it tore you apart. She should know, she'd been torn to shreds.

If her relationship with Crockett progressed and something happened to him or his children, she'd never survive. That was a risk she wasn't willing to take.

By the next morning, Crockett was a wreck. From the moment Mac had called him when he was on his way back to the castle yesterday, he'd been trying to find Paisley. He couldn't understand why she'd cancel her shopping trip with his daughter when she knew how much Mac had been looking forward to it. Backing out just didn't fit Paisley's MO.

But when Paisley never returned to the castle and wouldn't answer his calls, he began to worry. He'd even gone by her house multiple times, but she wasn't there. Or if she was, she didn't open the door.

Finally, he'd stopped by Rae's after hours, knowing Rae lived above the café, to ask if she'd heard from Paisley. She, too, tried calling, only to have it go straight to voice mail. They'd even called the shop over in Bluebird to see if she'd made it there to pick up her order. She had, but what happened to her after that was a mystery.

Worry had kept him awake most of the night. Had she had an accident? Was she lying in a ditch somewhere, injured? Had she been abducted? He watched the news enough to know that there was a whole lot of crazy in the world today.

As soon as Ashley arrived to watch the kids, he hightailed it into town, again calling Paisley's phone in hopes she would answer. When she didn't, he checked the castle first, then her house, only to discover nothing had changed since yesterday. Finally, he headed over to Rae's to see if she'd heard anything.

Standing behind the counter with a coffee-pot in her hand, she said, "I got a text from her about four this morning, letting me know that she wasn't feeling well and wouldn't be bringing any baked goods in today. I texted her back, but she never responded."

"So, if she was home, why wouldn't she answer the door?" And why hadn't she contacted him?

"Good question."

"Unless she was too sick to make it to the door." He hated the thought of her lying on the floor somewhere without anyone to help her.

"I gotta tell ya, Crockett, this's really got me perplexed." Rae looked at him rather strangely. "Did something happen between the two of you?"

Other than a couple of incredible kisses? "We didn't have an argument or anything if that's what you mean. On the contrary, she came out to the ranch Wednesday night and went horseback riding with me and the kids. Then we started demoing the kitchen at the castle yesterday morning, until we broke for lunch and she went to Bluebird and I ran to my office. We were getting along great." Better than great, actually. With the good Lord's help, Crockett had finally given in to his feelings for Paisley, and her response had him soaring to new heights.

"I'll try her again in a little while." Rae eyed the ranchers waiting to have their cups refilled.

"I'm going to run over there again." He hurried to the door, praying Paisley would let him in this time.

A few minutes later, he was on Paisley's porch, banging on her door. "I know you're in there, Paisley. Please, let me in so I can help you."

Sweat beaded his brow as the seconds ticked by until he heard the dead bolt click. He yanked the screen door open as she appeared in the doorway. Wearing gray yoga pants and a Bulldog sweatshirt, she peered up at him, those beautiful copper waves spilling over her shoulders in a tangled mess. She didn't look sick, but she didn't look like herself either.

"What's going on?" He stepped inside and closed the door behind him. "I've been worried about you. You didn't take my calls. I wish you'd let me know you were okay."

Her expression was almost vacant. Emotionless. He'd never seen her like this.

Arms crossed over her chest, she said, "I'm sorry I had to disappoint Mackenzie, but I just didn't think it was appropriate for her and me to make a trip like that."

"Why not? I mean, if it wasn't appropriate, why did you bring it up in the first place?"

"Things were different then. Between you and me."

His chest tightened as he stared into her sapphire eyes. "I don't get it."

"This—" she waved a hand between the two of them "—isn't going to work."

His heart tanked as a battle of emotions warred within him. "Funny, you seemed to be okay with it yesterday morning and the night before that. Then you go to pick up a gift and suddenly things aren't going to work? What changed, Paisley?"

"I did." Her gaze narrowed as she squared her shoulders. "I don't want a relationship with you outside of the castle."

Anger burned in his belly. He knew this scene all too well. He'd vowed to never watch it play out again and yet here he was. "Outside of the castle, huh?" Hands on his hips, he shook his head, realizing he'd been duped again. Sucked in by a beautiful woman with her own agenda. "I gotta hand it to you, Paisley. You're good. Even better than my ex."

She glared at him.

"Nothing you did or said was ever about me or my children, was it? Everything between us was an act just so you could fulfill your dream. You were willing to do anything to make that happen, weren't you? Even if you had to break some hearts along the way. Including those of a boy and girl who've already been through an emotional wringer. Well, you can count me out on the castle because I refuse to be manipulated again."

Turning, he jerked open the door and walked out of the house. He'd never imagined that he could be any angrier than he'd been when Shannon told him she was leaving, but he'd been wrong. Problem was, a good bit of that anger was directed at himself. How stupid could he be to allow himself to be fooled again?

He threw himself into his truck, fired up the engine and stepped on the gas so hard his tires squealed. Not that he cared. He just wanted to get as far away from Paisley Wainwright as possible. How foolish was he to think that she was interested in him? Instead, he'd been nothing but a pawn. She wanted the castle, and she was willing to do anything or use anyone to get it. She didn't care about him any more than his mother or Shannon had. Yet he'd fallen for her act.

When was he going to learn that he wasn't worth loving?

Chapter Sixteen

Paisley stood at her kitchen island later that afternoon, fixing a cup of honey-lavender tea. Every fiber of her being ached with grief. It was a feeling she knew well and had never wanted to experience again. In some ways this was worse than losing Peter and Logan because in trying to spare herself, she'd hurt others. Crockett, Mackenzie and David had found their way into her heart, and now she'd caused them pain, all because of her fear.

Suddenly, her motives seemed rather selfish. But what was done was done. She couldn't turn back now. Crockett would never forgive her. She just hoped the ache in her heart would subside someday, as it had before.

She removed the tea bag and set it aside, thinking about how quickly Crockett had drawn his own conclusions. He'd made her out to be worse than his ex-wife, and it stung. But then, that's what she wanted, wasn't it?

At what cost, though? His children would not only hate her, but believe they meant nothing to her. She'd seen how deep Crockett's wounds were from being abandoned by his mother and wife. Now she'd laid them wide open.

A knock sounded at her back door, and she looked up to see Christa and Laurel on her porch.

With a deep breath, she padded across the kitchen and opened the door. "What's going on?"

"We heard you weren't feeling well, so we came to check on you." Christa whisked past her with Laurel on her heels. "Rae would have come, too, but she didn't want to leave Maggie and Max."

Paisley closed the door. This was the first time she'd ever missed a day of baking for Rae, but she hadn't been able to muster the strength.

"We also heard that Crockett was frantically trying to find you." Laurel stopped beside the table, resting her hand atop her baby bump as she looked at Paisley. "Did he?"

Unwanted tears pricked Paisley's eyes as she nodded. She blinked them away, though.

"What's going on, Paise?" Arms crossed, her backside against the island, Christa watched her intently.

Along with Rae, these two women had become the closest friends Paisley had ever had. They knew her inside and out and loved her unconditionally. Hiding anything from them would be nearly impossible.

Too weary to stand, she grabbed her tea, moved to the table and pulled out a chair. "You two may as well join me."

They eased into the chairs on either side of her as she sipped her tea, watching her as they waited for her to lay out her troubles. But she didn't know where to begin. They weren't even aware that her relationship with Crockett had changed.

Drawing in a fortifying breath, she said, "Crockett and I have grown rather close in recent weeks."

"That's no surprise." Christa smiled. "I've seen how the two of you look at each other in church."

Paisley stared into her cup. "He kissed me. And I kissed him back."

"And?" Laurel leaned closer.

Paisley lifted a shoulder. "It was wonderful. And when we were working at the castle yesterday, everything was so easy and natural. The way a relationship is supposed to be. But then, something happened and all of the wonderful got drowned out by painful memories and more what-ifs than I can count."

Laurel reached for her hand. "What happened, Paisley?"

It took every ounce of energy she possessed to tell them about the accident and how it had dredged up unwanted memories and rattled her so intensely, causing her to cancel her trip with Mackenzie.

"All I could think of was what if I fall in love with Crockett and then lose him, too? Or if something were to happen to one of his kids?"

Christa pushed out of her chair, her face red as she began to pace the wooden floor. "First of all, there's no what-if about you loving Crockett. You're already there. Second—" she stopped and glared at Paisley "—what happened to the woman who preached to me about there being no fear in love?"

Paisley studied her half-empty cup. "She got a reality check."

"So just like that, you're going to let fear overrule your heart?" Christa was beside her now, anger burning in her hazel eyes. "You, the woman who adamantly called me out for being afraid of losing someone I loved. And, when I questioned you, you said it was 'better to have loved and lost than to never have loved at all.' How dare you?" Hands on her hips, she turned her back on Paisley to pace again.

"I knew you'd throw that in my face."

"Well, you know what?" Christa stopped and whirled to face her once again. "I'm glad I listened to you because if I'd have run away like I wanted to, I would have missed out on the best months of my life. Being a wife to Mick and a mom to Sadie has brought me more happiness than I ever thought possible. Yes, I'd be devastated if I lost either one of them, but I'd be so grateful for the memories of the time we had together."

Leaning back in her chair, Laurel watched her. "Paisley, you're the queen of romance. I don't understand why you'd be so quick to throw away a second chance when it's obvious you love Crockett. I would think you'd welcome it."

The tears she'd been battling began to fall. "Because I'm afraid. It took me forever to claw my way back to some semblance of normal after Peter and Logan died."

"And how did you do that?" Christa dropped into her seat.

Drawing in a shaky breath, Paisley said, "One step at a time, holding tightly to God's hand." She looked from Christa to Laurel then back at her cup as though it held the courage she so desperately needed right now. "Every time I thought I couldn't take another step, He urged me along. Even carried me."

Her expression softening, Christa took hold of Paisley's other hand. "Don't you see, sweetie? Now He's offering you a second chance. Not only at love, but to have a family. Do you really want to sacrifice that because of what could happen? This could be an opportunity for the happily-ever-after you always dreamed of."

She shook her head. "It's too late."

"What do you mean?" Christa's brow puckered. "How can it be too late?"

"Crockett was here earlier. I sent him away. Told him I didn't want a relationship with him outside of the castle." Her voice cracked as tears fell in earnest. "He was so angry. His poor heart has been so battered by his mother and his ex-wife. Now he thinks I'm just like them."

"Paisley—" Christa took her face into her hands "—can you look me in the eye and tell me that you're okay with letting the man you love and his children believe that you were only using them and that they mean nothing to you?"

In her mind, she could still see the pain in Crockett's eyes, hear the hurt in Mackenzie's voice when she'd dismissed her yesterday, and it killed her to think that it was all because of her.

"No. I love them all."

Christa's brow lifted. "Enough to put your own heart on the line?"

"But I'm so afraid." She sobbed. "What if they can't forgive me?"

Christa smiled as she released Paisley. "As a very wise woman once told me, if you let fear dictate your life, you might miss the greatest blessing ever."

"I don't know if Crockett will even talk to me." Paisley sniffed and dabbed at her eyes with her sleeves. "He was furious when he left. He's apt to slam the door in my face. And he certainly won't let me near his children." She looked at her two friends. "What should I do?"

"Well—" Laurel grinned "—I just might have an idea."

Crockett pulled up to the castle late Saturday morning, feeling more than a little rough. He should not be losing sleep over Paisley. Fortunately, her vehicle was nowhere to be found. When Wes called to say he needed to meet with him to discuss a potential problem at the castle, Crockett was afraid Paisley would be included.

He had yet to contact the Renwicks. He'd been too angry yesterday, so he'd decided to wait until next week, assuming he'd be calmer by then. He still found it difficult to believe that he'd been so wrong about Paisley. She'd actually made him believe they'd stumbled onto something special. He should have known it was too good to be true.

Wes's truck pulled in behind him, saving Crockett from his thoughts. He opened his door to greet the other man.

"Sorry to pull you away from your kids on a Saturday, but this is kind of important."

"Not a problem. They each spent the night with friends last night." Something he was more than grateful for, particularly in Mac's case. He'd rather she enjoy time with her friends instead of sitting around the house moping.

"I am curious about this potential problem, though." He unlocked the door, and they stepped inside. "You haven't even started working yet."

"Follow me." Wes continued to the staircase. "The issue is in the ballroom."

Crockett trudged behind Wes, trying to concentrate on the castle and not Paisley's dismissal.

"You know, sometimes things aren't quite what they seem," Wes said. "They're crafted to look in a way that's contrary to the true character."

Like the way Paisley had fooled him. And he'd fallen for every bit of her act.

When they rounded into the ballroom, Crockett stopped in his tracks. There, in the middle of the room, was Paisley, wearing the same sundress she'd worn the night of the reception. The night he realized he was falling for her.

"What are you doing here?"

She strode toward them. "I need to talk to you. But I was pretty sure you'd shut down any attempt to do that." She called that right.

Cutting a look at Wes, he said, "You knew about this?"

"Just hear her out, all right?" As Wes turned to leave, he set a hand on Crockett's shoulder. "Do yourself a favor and listen with your heart, not your head." He disappeared as Paisley drew closer.

Crockett had never been more tempted to turn tail and run, but his feet felt as though they were cemented to the floor.

Her gaze seemed riveted to his. "I owe you an apology."

"Save it. I can't believe anything you say anyway."

She stopped in front of him. "Everything I've ever told you was the truth."

"Yeah, right." He rubbed the back of his neck. "Until the other day."

His gaze narrowed as Wes's parting words repeated in his mind. *Listen with your heart, not your head.*

He lowered his arm. "Go on."

"The only thing I lied about was when I said I didn't want a relationship with you outside of the castle. And then I allowed you to believe the worst."

"That doesn't make any sense." Of course, it could be his lack of sleep.

"When I was on my way back from Bluebird,

I was sideswiped by a truck on the highway, and I almost lost control."

Despite her treating him as though he were nothing more than a pawn in her quest for the castle, the urge to comfort her swelled inside of him. He longed to reach for her. Hold her. And he hated it.

"By the time I made it to the shoulder, my head was swimming with images of Peter's mangled car. And then Mackenzie called, and I suddenly realized that, if something were to happen on our way to the city, I might not be able to protect her. I was scared, so scared that I convinced myself it wasn't safe to take her. So I made up some flimsy excuse not to." Her eyes shimmered with unshed tears. "The disappointment in her voice tore a hole right through me, but I kept telling myself that I was doing it to protect her. Then I thought about you."

His heart stopped as he waited for her to continue.

"When you kissed me the other night, my heart soared. It told me that whatever was going on between us wasn't one-sided. That you had opened yourself up to the possibility of a relationship with me." She hung her head. "Yet as I sat on the side of that busy road, reliving all of the pain and agony I went through after Peter and Logan died, I thought of how devastated you would be if something happened to the kids." A tear spilled onto her cheek. "I didn't want either of us to have to experience that kind of pain."

She sniffed, making eye contact once again. "It's funny, as I tell you this, it all sounds so lame. But in the aftermath of that sideswipe, the memories of what I went through when I lost Peter and Logan were so vivid. There were days when I didn't think I could go on. And others when I didn't want to."

He couldn't stop himself from pulling her into his arms.

"I'm sorry I lied to Mackenzie." She sobbed, her tears seeping through his shirt and into his heart. "I owe her an apology." Pulling away, she squared her shoulders. "One I fully intend to give her, if you'll allow me."

Emotions warred inside of him as his mind struggled to grasp all she was telling him.

She looked him in the eye. "I should have told you all of this the other day and given you the opportunity to help me overcome my fears the way you've overcome yours. But I didn't. Instead, I foolishly believed that it would be easier to have you hate me than to risk seeing you go through what I did. I was wrong." Her tears fell anew. "I love you, Crockett."

Closing his eyes, he entwined their fingers and rested his forehead against hers, allowing her words to wash over him and erase all of the pain and doubt. She was telling him the truth. He knew it in his heart.

After a long moment, he cradled her face in his hands and looked into her sapphire eyes. "You are, without a doubt, the most beautiful woman I have ever had the pleasure of knowing. But it's your inner beauty that made me love you, Paisley. You're caring, selfless, nurturing." He brushed away her tears with his thumbs. "You make me want to throw off my fears and explore a future with you."

Taking his hands in hers, she gave a soft laugh. "You know, I once thought of you as heartless. Then I realized that you were merely hiding behind that battle-worn armor so you wouldn't be hurt again. And every once in a while, I'd catch a glimpse of the prince that was inside, the one who loves his children unconditionally and longs to be loved himself." She looked deep into his eyes. "Shannon and your mother were the ones with the problem, Crockett. Not you. They were so absorbed in themselves that they never took the time to notice how special you are and how much love you deserve."

His Adam's apple bobbed as his eyes searched hers. "You really believe that?"

"With all of my heart. And the idea of exploring a future with you sounds like a dream come true."

He kissed her then, feeling as though he'd finally been set free of the lies that had held him captive for so long.

Dad was right. With God, all things really were possible. Crockett was tired of wrestling. God had heard the desires of his heart and given him a second chance. And perhaps, one day, he would have the family he'd always dreamed of.

Epilogue

The first Saturday in November was, by far, the most glorious day of this entire year. A year marked by a freak ice storm and near-record floods had ebbed into a delightful fall with mild temperatures and brilliant blue skies. Paisley couldn't be more pleased. This was the perfect day for the residents of Bliss to get a sneak peek at the Bliss Texas History Museum and Event Center at Renwick Castle.

Sun filtered through the leaves of a large live oak as she moved through the series of tables adorned with greenery, branches, pumpkins and gourds, making sure everything was just so. The castle grounds had been beautifully landscaped and locals had been abuzz for weeks, anticipation growing for the event that was set to be a party for the whole town.

"Paisley, my dear—" Molly Renwick Simmons stepped off of the terrace with her cousin,

Jared, who'd accompanied her for the event "—this is absolutely stunning." She adjusted her flowing kimono-style cardigan. "It has the look of an autumnal garden party."

Paisley approached the two. "I'm pleased to hear you say that because a garden party was just the look I was going for. I mean, this is a castle, after all."

"With a Texas flare." Jared, who looked close to Molly's age, though he was much quieter, nodded toward the food tables where chili and corn muffins would be served, along with an assortment of cookies.

"And thanks to you and Crockett," Molly gushed, "we can now share it with the world."

Paisley looked from the woman to Jared. "Well, we couldn't have done it without you, so thank you."

Checking her watch, Molly said, "The gates will open in thirty minutes. Are you ready?"

"I believe so. I need to round up Crockett and our families, though." Paisley's parents, along with Dale and Irene, had come in for the event and were exploring the castle with the kids before the crowds arrived. "I'm sure he's still putzing around the museum. No matter how many times I tell him things are perfect, he keeps moving stuff around."

"The man has a vision." Molly tapped the side

of her head. "He wants to make sure he's translated it correctly."

"Indeed, he does."

"Why don't you run along and see about everyone while Jared and I make sure everything is ready out here."

"Thank you. I will do that." Paisley smoothed a hand over her deep green sheath dress as she moved onto the terrace and through the open French doors, smiling as her gaze roamed the renovated space. Other than the kitchen, most of the rooms had merely been refreshed and repurposed. Gone was the musty odor. Luster had been restored to the mahogany panels and ceiling while the limestone walls and floors had been cleaned and sealed, making everything look crisp and fresh.

She continued up the entry hall, past the dining room with its gleaming display cases filled with artifacts from Crockett's collection, eyeing the knight's armor that once again stood sentry near the front door. A perfect way to set the stage for the two fairy-tale weddings already booked for next spring.

Hearing voices coming from what had been the family room, she made a left turn into the space that was now dedicated to the Battle of the Alamo. Crockett, Dale and her father huddled near a display case along the far wall.

"And what sort of mischief are you three cooking up?"

They startled as she continued toward them, looking as though they'd been caught stealing from the cookie jar.

Stuffing his hands into the pockets of his black dress slacks, Crockett cleared his throat. "I was, uh, just showing them this old rifle." He gestured to the case behind him.

Her brow lifted as she approached the trio. "Then why do you look so guilty?"

The three men glanced at each other before her father said, "Yeah, you caught us in here havin' fun while you were outside workin'." He looked at Crockett's father. "Dale, we'd best go find our wives."

Watching the two men retreat, Crockett called after them. "Better tell the kids to come on, too."

Paisley moved beside the man she loved so much, surveying the room now filled with displays of everything from weapons to books and letters to portraits and maps. The museum had been a labor of love for Crockett as he worked to bring his grandfather's dream to life, and it had turned out beautifully. Now if she could only convince him.

"You did an amazing job with the museum, Crockett. Your grandfather would be proud."

Wrapping an arm around her waist, he tugged

her close and gave her a brief kiss. "Thank you for saying that."

She drew in a breath, savoring this moment alone. "I can't believe this day is finally here."

"I know." He smiled down at her. "Everything came together just the way we planned."

"I think we make a pretty good team."

"We sure do." He lowered his head one more time as the children's voices echoed through the entry hall. "I guess it's time to get this show on the road."

Soon, they were standing in front of the castle with Mackenzie, David, Molly and Jared, waving as townsfolk flooded through the gates. Since they were expecting a large crowd, residents were instructed to park at the high school then brought to the castle via school bus. It took a while to get everyone inside the castle walls, but once they did, Paisley, Crockett and the rest of them moved to the terrace to address the crowd and invite them to tour the castle.

"Hello, Bliss!" Crockett bellowed into a microphone just before three o'clock, setting off a round of thunderous applause.

Paisley stood to his right while Mackenzie and David were beside and in front of her wearing the biggest smiles ever. By the grace of God, Crockett's daughter had readily forgiven Paisley for breaking her promise, and their relationship—

which included regular shopping trips—had continued to grow since.

Once the throng of people quieted, Crockett reached for Paisley's hand, and she proudly took hold. "This lovely lady and I would like to thank all of you for joining us to celebrate the new Bliss Texas History Museum and Event Center at Renwick Castle."

More applause erupted, infused with a few whistles.

"You know, this old castle has been sitting here forgotten and overlooked for a long time, but Paisley and I had a dream. Not the same dream, mind you—" he winked at her, making her heart flutter "—just something that had each of us contacting the Renwick family." Letting go of her hand, he motioned Molly and Jared forward. "Y'all give a big Bliss welcome to Mr. Jared Renwick and Mrs. Molly Renwick Simmons."

The cousins waved as people cheered.

"Thanks to the generosity of the Renwick family," Crockett continued, "Paisley and I, along with a host of helpers—" he pointed to Wes, who was holding four-month-old Wyatt "—have managed to breathe new life into this spectacular piece of Texas history."

Glancing at Paisley, he went on. "For those of you who know Paisley and me, you're aware what an unlikely pairing we were. Yet with a common goal of giving this castle a new lease on life, we made it work. What we hadn't expected was that it would be the beginning of something new in our lives."

He again reached for Paisley's hand, drawing her closer. "Paisley, I want to thank you for partnering with me on this adventure. It turned out better than I could have imagined, and that's only because of you." His expression turned serious as he twisted toward Molly and held out the microphone. "Would you hold this for me, please?"

As a breeze sifted across the castle grounds, sparking chill bumps on Paisley's arms, Crockett shoved a hand into his pocket. Before she could wrap her brain around what was happening, he dropped to one knee in front of her.

A few whoops came from townsfolk before everyone went silent.

With a wide smile, Crockett looked up at her. "Paisley Wainwright, will you marry me?"

She didn't have to think. She knew beyond a shadow of a doubt that she wanted to share her life with this man and his two beautiful children. "Oh, yes!"

Applause, whoops and whistles filled her ears as Crockett stood and slid the cushion-cut diamond on her left hand as Mackenzie and David moved beside them.

"This is so cool!" Mackenzie hugged her.

David wrapped his arms around Paisley's waist and peered up at her. "Does this mean I finally get to have a mom?"

Tears pricked her eyes as she hugged Crockett's son. "Darlin', I would be honored."

Crockett teasingly nudged his children out of the way. "Hold on, guys. I've still gotta seal this deal." His arm snaked around Paisley's waist and pulled her close. "I love you, Paisley. You've shown me the true meaning of love and made me believe that I might actually be worthy of it."

Laying a hand on either side of his face, she couldn't seem to stop smiling. "My sweet Crockett. You are worthy of so much love. I will cherish you always."

Finally, he kissed her. This misunderstood man who'd unexpectedly captured her heart.

Five years ago, Paisley never imagined her life could be this full again. But God had a plan to bring two wounded hearts together and make them one. To teach them that love really does conquer all and grant them a second chance at forever. Together, they'd learned to face their fears, overcome obstacles and, ultimately, discovered an abiding love and respect for one other.

Through the fog of euphoria, she heard Molly say, "I think I might know of a great place for a wedding."

* * * * *

Dear Reader,

There's something very satisfying when people find love again after having lost a spouse, either through death or divorce. It's almost as if they have a deeper appreciation for a romantic relationship, even though they may be reluctant to give in to it. Paisley and Crockett deserved to find each other. She was worthy of a happily-ever-after, and Crockett needed to experience unconditional love. to know he was loved and believe he was worthy of it.

And what better way to bring these two unlikely souls together than a castle. The idea came when someone reminded me there had once been a castle on the banks of the river in our little town. Sadly, that castle is no more, having been compromised by a flood in the late 1800s, but, as often happens with writers, I began to think, *What if?* What if that castle had survived? There are actually many castles throughout the United States. And so, Renwick Castle was born.

Thank you for joining me on this third pass through the town of Bliss, Texas. Laurel's and Christa's stories were books one and two in the series. Our fourth and final story belongs to Rae. I can't wait to see what's in store for the sweet café owner with a heart as big as Texas.

In the meantime, I would love to hear from

you. You can contact me via my website, mindyobenhaus.com, or you can snail-mail me c/o Love Inspired Books, 195 Broadway, 24th Floor, New York, NY 10007.

Wishing you many blessings,
Mindy

Get 4 FREE REWARDS!

We'll send you 2 FREE Books plus 2 FREE Mystery Gifts.

Love Inspired books feature uplifting stories where faith helps guide you through life's challenges and discover the promise of a new beginning.

FREE
Value Over
$20

Get 4 FREE REWARDS!

We'll send you 2 FREE Books plus 2 FREE Mystery Gifts.

Harlequin Heartwarming Larger-Print books will connect you to uplifting stories where the bonds of friendship, family and community unite.

FREE Value Over **$20**

HARLEQUIN SELECTS COLLECTION

From Robyn Carr to RaeAnne Thayne to Linda Lael Miller and Sherryl Woods we promise (actually, GUARANTEE!) each author in the Harlequin Selects collection has seen their name on the *New York Times* or *USA TODAY* bestseller lists!

COMING NEXT MONTH FROM
Love Inspired

AN UNEXPECTED AMISH HARVEST
The Amish of New Hope • by Carrie Lighte
When Susannah Peachy returns to her grandfather's potato farm to help out after her grandmother is injured, she's not ready to face Peter Lambright—the Amish bachelor who broke her heart. But she doesn't know his reason for ending things...and the truth could make all the difference for their future.

THE COWBOY'S AMISH HAVEN
by Pamela Desmond Wright
With three sisters to look after and her family ranch falling into foreclosure, Gail Schroder turns to her childhood sweetheart, Levi Wyse, to help her learn the cattle business. But can the cowboy teach this Amish spinster the ropes in time to save her home?

A MOTHER'S STRENGTH
Wander Canyon • by Allie Pleiter
Molly Kane will do anything to help her son overcome his anxieties—including enlisting Sawyer Bradshaw to give him golf lessons. But as the little boy draws them together, can Molly and Sawyer also heal each other's hearts?

LOST AND FOUND FAITH
by Laurel Blount
Changed by the grief of losing his wife, Neil Hamilton's no longer the caring teacher he once was—until a two-year-old boy shows up on his doorstep and opens his heart. Helping little Oliver bond with his adoptive mother, Maggie Byrne, might just restore Neil's faith...and give him hope for the future.

CHASING HER DREAM
by Jennifer Slattery
Returning home to run her late uncle's ranch, single mom Rheanna Stone never expected the operation to be in such disarray...or that she'd need to rely on the cowboy who once left her behind. But if she wants to save it, Dave Brewster's her only hope—even if it means risking her heart all over again.

THE BULL RIDER'S FRESH START
by Heidi McCahan
After former champion bull rider Landon Chambers's friends are killed in a car accident, the baby they were temporarily caring for needs him. But when Kelsey Sinclair returns from her deployment to claim her daughter, he's shocked to learn *he's* the father...and he's not ready to let either of them go.

LICNM0821